Shandra Higheagle Mystery Books

Double Duplicity

Tarnished Remains

Deadly Aim

Murderous Secrets

Killer Descent

Reservation Revenge

Yuletide Slaying

Fatal Fall

Haunting Corpse

Shandra Higheagle Mystery

Paty Jager

Windtree Press

Hillsboro, Or

Special Thanks

To my awesome critique and editing team. Stephanie, Karen, Maggie, and Angie. Without you ladies this and many other books would not be as pleasurable to read.

Chapter One

Shandra Higheagle finished poking white baby's breath into her friend Ruthie Kerby's hair. The large tube curls in her usual afro and the flapper style white wedding dress, gave the bride the look of a gangster's songbird from a 1920s movie.

"Maxwell is going to faint when he sees you," Shandra said, hugging her friend. "I still can't believe you two are finally getting married and I get to be your maid of honor." Shandra swung her hips, making the fringe on her red flapper dress swing.

Ruthie laughed. "Maxwell was beginning to wonder if this would ever happen as well." She peered at a spot above the floor length mirror in Shandra's bedroom. "I've only told Maxwell this, but I never intended to marry and have kids." Her gaze landed on Shandra. "You can't trust a man to stay when the going gets tough."

Shandra shook her head. "There are many men who do stick around. Look at Ryan, and Dr. Porter, and even

Maxwell. He's hung out a lot of years waiting for you to finally give in. I think that means a lot."

A soft smile tipped Ruthie's full lips and her eyes sparkled. "Yeah, he has proven he's not going anywhere."

A soft knock and the door opened. Naomi Norton, another close friend, stuck her head in. "There's someone here who wants to see the bride."

"Not Maxwell!" Ruthie cried, ducking behind the full-length mirror. "That's bad luck."

Naomi shook her head. "It's your mother."

Ruthie's eyes narrowed. "My mother? I didn't tell her—"

A thin, crinkle skinned, African American woman with more gray than black in her short dreadlocks, stepped in the door. "Your wonderful young man invited me." The woman's voice was stronger than her appearance.

"He had no right. If I wanted you here, I would have invited you myself." Ruthie didn't budge from her spot behind the mirror as if she needed it to shield her from the woman.

"You are beautiful. I always knew you would grow up to be a beauty like your grandmother." Mrs. Kerby didn't appear to take the hint she wasn't wanted.

"Why don't you wait to reminisce until after the wedding," Shandra said, steering the older woman back toward the door.

For a woman who looked so frail, she dug her feet in and wouldn't be budged. "I came to tell my daughter I'm sorry for the years I lost to drinking. I'm sorry for the years I wasn't there for you."

"You left me on Nattie's doorstep. You didn't want to be there for me after Daddy left. You abandoned me just like he did." Ruthie's voice no longer sounded grownup.

Shandra had never seen her always cheerful, upbeat friend look so sad and lost.

"Mrs. Kerby, you'll have to leave." Shandra physically grabbed the woman by the arm, led her to the door, shoved her out, and closed her away from Ruthie.

She crossed the room and put an arm around her friend's shoulders. "Are you okay?"

"What was he thinking inviting her?" The lost little girl was now a fuming woman. "How could he invite someone I told him I didn't want here?"

"I'm sure it was a loving gesture on Maxwell's part." Shandra tried to soothe her friend.

Naomi stuck her head in the door. "Ten minutes." She peered at them and entered the room. "What's wrong?"

"It wasn't a warm reunion," Shandra said, handing Ruthie tissues to keep her tears from ruining her make-up.

"Oh! I'm sorry! If I'd know that I wouldn't have allowed her to come see you." Now Naomi had tears glistening in her eyes. She plucked tissue from the box and dabbed.

"Take a deep breath. Maxwell didn't bring your mother here to upset you or the wedding. He's been waiting a long time to make you Mrs. Maxwell Treat," Shandra said, picking up the small bridal bouquet of red and white roses. She was glad that while Ruthie and Maxwell had picked the 1920s for the theme of their wedding, they hadn't gone with a gruesome Halloween theme to go with the holiday coming up in four days.

Ruthie breathed in deep and took the bouquet.

Naomi smiled. "Come on, Maid of Honor, you need to take your place." Her eyes sparkled. "You are going to make Ryan's pinstripes stand up and take notice."

Shandra grinned. Ryan had reluctantly agreed to be Maxwell's best man, only because Ruthie had insisted he wouldn't want any other man being paired with Shandra once he got an eyeful of her dress.

"I'll see you in the barn." Shandra gave Ruthie a hug. "Maxwell's eyes are going to pop when he sees you."

Naomi led the way out of the bedroom and walked with Shandra across the area from her house to the barn. A wedding planner had arrived the day before and set up chairs, tables, and an altar in the barn. Maxwell's family was small and Ruthie only had Nattie, the Indian woman who took her in and her daughter, Chea, whom she'd invited. Her mother also sat on the bride's side, looking fidgety.

Naomi stood to the side as Ryan stepped up and took Shandra's arm.

"You are stunning," he whispered as they walked down the aisle together.

"You're not too bad yourself, gangster," she retorted. She glanced up at Maxwell waiting nervously beside the preacher.

She gave him a smile and a thumbs up.

He nodded back and stared down the aisle.

The song *At Last* by Etta James began. The two had picked this over the traditional wedding march.

Everyone stood and faced the open barn doors.

The song played on, but the bride didn't arrive. Shandra caught a glimpse of the back of a man ducking behind the studio as Naomi hurried as fast as she could in heels to the house.

The song ended.

No Ruthie in her white flapper dress.

Maxwell strode down the aisle, his head pivoted toward Mrs. Kerby before he took out of the barn at a lope.

Shandra kicked off her heels and ran after him. The pounding of feet behind her told her Ryan was right behind.

Shandra hurried through the front door.

Naomi stood at the bedroom doorway looking overwrought.

"Where's Ruthie?" Shandra asked as Maxwell charged out of the bedroom.

"Where did she go?" Maxwell shouted.

His shout caused Naomi to burst into tears. "I don't know."

"Yelling at Naomi isn't going to tell us anything," Ryan said, putting an arm around Maxwell's shoulders and leading him to a dining room chair.

"Did you see the man?" Shandra asked Naomi.

Maxwell's head popped up. "What man?"

"When Naomi was headed to the house to get Ruthie, I spotted a man ducking down the side of the studio."

Ryan jumped to his feet. "I'll check it out."

Maxwell surged to his feet. "I'm coming."

"No, you're not. You stay here and see if you and Shandra can figure out what happened. She was with Ruthie up until she walked to the barn." Ryan kissed her temple and whispered, "Keep him calm."

She nodded. "Naomi, why don't you go let the guests know there is a bit of a delay."

Her friend nodded, and dabbing her eyes, walked out of the house.

"Why did you invite Ruthie's mother against her wishes?" Shandra decided to start in with what had upset her friend.

Maxwell had the decency to give her a sheepish glance. "I thought her mother should be at her wedding. We talked about it. I told her family should be at weddings. She said her only family was invited. Meaning Nattie and Chea."

"Her mother came into the house before the wedding to try and talk with Ruthie."

His eyes widened, making a stark white contrast to his mahogany skin. "You think that's why she didn't show up? She's mad at me for inviting her mother?"

"I don't know. I had her talked out of being mad at you when I left the room." She wandered into the kitchen and brought them both back a glass of water.

He took the glass and downed half in one gulp. He wiped the back of his hand across his mouth and peered at her. "Do you think I ruined my own wedding?"

She shook her head. "We won't know until we find Ruthie and know what she's thinking." Shandra sat on the couch next to Maxwell. "What I gathered from Ruthie's conversation with her mother, Mrs. Kerby abandoned her after her father left."

"Yeah. She's felt like no one could love her. I know she kept putting the wedding off, thinking I'd leave her, too." His eyes sparkled and his voice went warm. "I'll never leave her. She makes me happy just thinking about her. I like that I can chase her doldrums away and make her laugh." He sighed. "She has the best laugh."

Shandra smiled. This man would never do anything to lose Ruthie. His need to have family at the wedding had pushed him to invite the unwanted mother.

Ryan came through the still open front door. "I can't

find any sign of the man or Ruthie."

Shandra stood. "I guess I better tell the guests there won't be a wedding today."

Chapter Two

Two hours after the wedding was to start, the guests had all left. Naomi and Ted stayed to help clean up the chairs and streamers. Shandra didn't see any sense in waiting for the crew the wedding planner had hired. They weren't to show up until tomorrow.

"That was a short wedding," Lil, Shandra's employee, said. The woman came with the ranch like the stray cat usually around the eccentric woman's neck.

"There wasn't a wedding. The bride got cold feet," Ted said.

"I don't know if it was cold feet or that she needed to deal with the shock of her mother caring before she could get married," Shandra said, stacking chairs. Sheba, her pony-sized mutt, followed her back and forth as if afraid she would get locked up in the studio again. It had been the consensus of everyone involved in the wedding plans to leave the clumsy dog in the studio during the wedding. No one had wanted her to knock over guests, food, or cake.

Ryan stacked the two chairs he had and faced Lil. "Did you happen to see anyone milling around behind the studio or barn before the wedding?"

"Wouldn't know. I was bent over the glazing table glazing coasters." She wadded up the red streamers she'd pulled from the rafters. "Didn't know anything was wrong until I heard the cars start up and knew it was too early for the reception to be over."

Shandra folded two more chairs and carried them over to stack along the wall. "It doesn't make sense. Ruthie was smiling and ready to marry Maxwell when I left the room. There wasn't that much time between when I left and Naomi went looking for Ruthie."

"She had to have gone out through the forest." Ryan said, placing two more chairs in the stack. "All the vehicles were accounted for."

"What would make her run out through the forest?" Shandra stared out the barn doors to the trees surrounding her meadow. "Do you think she went to their new house? It's only four miles down the road from here?"

"I'd think that would be the first place Maxwell would look for her," Ryan said.

"I feel like we aren't doing enough. We should be looking for her." Shandra had a bad feeling about her friend. And what about the man she'd seen? "You didn't see any footprints or anything when you looked behind the studio?"

Ryan stopped folding chairs and shook his head. "I didn't see anything unusual."

"Then where did that man go?"

"Lewis, where have you been?" Lil walked toward the side of the barn where Lewis, her orange cat sat. "What's this? Where did you get red paint?"

"Don't touch!" Ryan said, striding across the barn to the cat. "I don't think that's paint."

Shandra knelt beside Lewis. Fear tingled her spine. Sheba sniffed at the cat who hunched his back and hissed. "I don't think so either. Lewis rubbed up against someone who is bleeding." Her chest constricted. "Ruthie!"

Ryan took photos of Lewis with his phone. If this turned into a homicide he'd need more than photos of the cat. "Lil, put the cat in your room and Sheba back in the studio." He walked to the barn doors. "Everyone spread out and look for what this cat rubbed up against." If they were lucky they'd discover one of the horses had injured themselves. But with the events of the day, his gut said they were looking for a person. He saw the panic in Shandra's eyes thinking it could be her friend. If it was Ruthie, they needed to find her and get to the bottom of her disappearance.

"Shandra, you look around the house. Ted, Naomi, you look around the studio." Ryan strode along the side of the barn scanning for signs of blood or a struggle. He glanced at the corral and noticed the horses all staring at something on the far side. Stepping up on a rail, he climbed over the fence and crossed the corral.

He stopped short at the sight of an arm hanging over the bottom rail of the fence. It wasn't Ruthie. The hand was too large, and she wouldn't have been wearing an army jacket.

Ryan climbed over the fence. One look and he knew the man was gone. Someone had knocked him alongside the head good enough to tear his ear and skin and spill a lot of blood. He placed his fingers on the man's carotid artery but didn't feel a pulse. The body wasn't cold, the blood still dripped from his head wound.

He pulled out his phone and dialed the county dispatch.

"Hey Ryan, I thought you were in a wedding today," his oldest sister, Cathleen, said. That was the problem with having a sibling working the county dispatch when you were a detective with the sheriff's department. You couldn't get away from your family.

"Wedding didn't happen. I just discovered a body behind Shandra's barn."

"Another body at Shandra's? Are you sure you want to marry that woman?"

He understood his sister's concerns. While Shandra believed this ranch to be her bounty, having the clay she used in her pottery, he was beginning to think it and the mountain that housed the ranch were cursed. There had been too many bodies found here in recent years.

"I'm marrying the woman, not the mountain."

"But you two plan to live there after the wedding." Cathleen always liked to see the cup half empty rather than half full.

"What matters now is I need a couple of deputies, the ME, and an ambulance out here." He would deal with the fallout from his family about a death on Shandra's property later.

"On their way," Cathleen said.

Ryan hung up the phone as Shandra, Ted, and Naomi came around the side of the barn.

"What did you find?" Shandra asked, climbing over the fence.

"Stay there. It's not Ruthie. It's a man." Using the

handkerchief dangling from the breast pocket of his pinstripe suit, he put his hand into the man's back pocket and pulled out a wallet. With a flip, it opened and the man's face stared back at him from an Oregon driver's license. Donald Kerby.

"Who is he?" Shandra asked, sitting on the top of the fence. The Nortons stood beside her.

"From the birthdate and the name, I would surmise he is, or was, Ruthie's father." Ryan didn't like this at all. The man found dead and most likely killed about the time that Ruthie came up missing.

Chapter Three

Shandra felt her body tense. "Where are you Ruthie?" she whispered. At a time like this she wished her deceased grandmother would come to her out of the blue instead of in dreams. If she could communicate with Ella when she was awake, Shandra could ask her where to find Ruthie.

This wasn't a good sign that a man Ryan presumed was Ruthie's father was killed and she was missing.

Ryan stood. "Now I wish we hadn't sent everyone home." He glanced her direction. "Do you have a list of the guests?"

"No, but I'm sure Maxwell can call them, most were local, except for Ruthie's mom."

"That's who I'd like to see first." Ryan waved a hand at the dead man. "I have to stay here, now that I found the body. Shandra, would you go to my work SUV and get my forensics kit?"

She nodded and climbed down off the fence and faced her friends. "Why don't you two go in the house and get some coffee going. Naomi, pull out the reception food. We can feed the police who show up."

The couple nodded, and walking close together, headed to the house.

Shandra hurried between the barn and the studio toward the far side of the house where they had parked the tractor, her jeep, and Ryan's work vehicle and his pickup. They hadn't moved his vintage car to the ranch yet.

She knew which backpack in the SUV Ryan wanted. It seemed since meeting him, all she managed to do was get caught up in murders. They'd met when she was a suspect in the killing of a gallery owner, and she'd been a suspect when her ex-lover ended up dead at Huckleberry Ski Resort. She sighed. This time she couldn't be a suspect. But she feared for her friend.

Ruthie didn't have an alibi, and she'd look even guiltier if the man did turn out to be her estranged father.

A jazz tune tinkled from Shandra's phone.

"Hello?"

"It's Maxwell. I found Ruthie. She's curled up in a ball on her bed above the restaurant. She's covered in scratches and won't talk to me." The pain in his voice tugged at Shandra.

"Don't touch her or do anything. I'll be there as soon as I can. But Maxwell, we found a body by the corrals. Ryan thinks it's Ruthie's father."

The big man on the other end of the conversation, cursed. She'd never heard him say the words the like of which came from him now.

"Maxwell. Keep her there and keep her calm. Don't say anything until we are sure." She could feel the man's agitation through his silence. "Maxwell. Did you hear me?"

"Yes. She didn't do it. Ruthie wouldn't hurt a fly."

"I know. Wait for me. I'll be there as soon as I can." She hung up the phone and jogged the backpack over to Ryan.

Her first glimpse of the dead man, he looked as if he were sitting with his back to the corral.

"Don't come any further." Ryan met her, taking the pack.

"Maxwell called. He found Ruthie curled up on her bed above the diner. I want to go talk to her." She peered into Ryan's eyes, hoping he understood her need to be there for her friend.

"Did you tell him about the body?"

"Yes. But I also said we weren't sure it was her father and to not tell her." Shandra had butted into enough of Ryan's investigations since meeting him to know she had to tell him everything she did or said. It was the only way to keep him from getting into trouble with his superiors. He believed in her dreams and her grandmother. Those dreams had helped solve several murders.

"You can go, but tell Ted and Naomi to stick around. It will be easier to keep this contained if the people who know aren't running around spreading what they've seen." Ryan unzipped the outside pocket on the pack and started snapping photos. "When I finish here, I want to get photos and samples of the blood on the cat."

"If Lewis hasn't licked the blood off already." She stated what was obvious. The feline wasn't likely to remain dirty for long.

Ryan's gaze snapped around to her. "True. Times like this I wish you didn't live so far from everything. It takes too long for law enforcement to get here." He glanced to the barn. "Have Lil bring Lewis out here so I can take more photos now that I know it is a homicide. I can't leave the crime scene. It's too fresh to have someone come along and muck things up."

She walked over and kissed him on the cheek.

"Not that I mind, but what's that for?" His all business manner softened.

"Because you understand I need to be with Ruthie." She spun on her heel and strode along the side of the barn and through the open doors. At the tack room, she knocked once and entered. Lil had refused to move into the apartment above the studio. She claimed she preferred living in the tack room. Shandra had a notion it was because in the tack room she didn't have to be neat and could smell the leather and horses.

"Police comin'?" Lil asked, holding Lewis on her lap. There was still blood on his fur.

"Yes."

"Then you found a body." Lil's spiked white hair stuck out from her head like a cat that had been dunked in water. She wore a purple paisley blouse, purple jeans, and had on the purple cowgirl boots Shandra had given her for Christmas the year before.

"Ryan did. He can't leave the body alone until reinforcements arrive and he would like you to bring Lewis out so he can get more photos." She put her hand on the door handle. "I'm headed to Ruthie's. Maxwell found her in her place above the diner."

Lil squinted one eye and stared at her. "What aren't you tellin' me?"

"We think the dead person is Ruthie's father who left when she was ten."

"Donald Kerby?"

"Yes. You knew him?" Shandra should have realized Lil would know the man. She'd lived in Weippe County all her sixty plus years.

"He was the star basketball player for Warner High back in the seventies. He married Ruthie's mom and never went on to college." Lil stood, draping Lewis around her neck like a mink stole. The blood smeared side of him up.

"Any idea why he left Ruthie and her mom?" Shandra was curious to know this before getting a little girl's version.

"He was known to like the ladies. I always figured he found someone to shack up with who didn't care if they married. As far as I know, he never divorced Zelda."

"Thanks." Shandra walked out of the barn and climbed into her Jeep.

Out on the country road she passed two county cars and a state police car with their lights and sirens going.

~*~

Ryan had known Shandra would go to Ruthie's aid as soon as the woman was found. What he feared was her friend had killed her father.

Lil approached him with the orange cat around her neck. No matter how many times he'd seen the woman wearing the cat this way, he still found it fascinating to watch the animal lounge around her neck.

"Shandra must have told you I need more photos of Lewis now that this is a homicide."

"Yeah." Lil removed the animal from her shoulders and set him on the ground, keeping hold of his scruff. "Don't want him runnin' off before you get your pictures."

"I'll get those photos now." He took photos from three

to four feet away from the animal, getting a disgusted look from both the animal and the owner.

When he finished, Lil released the cat and stood, studying the deceased. "Yep. That's Donald."

"You knew the man?" Ryan pulled out his notepad and poised his pen.

"He was in school a little behind me. Good ball player."

"Have you seen him lately?" Ryan had to figure out how the man had known about his daughter's wedding when it was believed the man had disappeared.

"No. Not since he walked out on Zelda and Ruthie. Couldn't blame the man for walking out on Zelda, but I never did figure out why he didn't take Ruthie with him." Lil turned from the man and leaned her arms over the top railing of the corral.

"Why did he leave his wife?"

"Back then she was a mess. Sloppy drunk and word was she was taking drugs, too. Can't blame him for walkin' away from that, but leavin' poor Ruthie with that woman… That didn't sound like Donald."

"Anyone say where he went?" Ryan wasn't liking the scenario of this man coming back into Ruthie's life right now.

"Speculation."

"His driver's license said Medford, Oregon. He have any relatives there?" The man had to have a reason to move to another state so far from his child.

"Can't remember."

Shrill sirens invaded the tranquil mountain setting.

"Would you direct the officers back here, please?" Ryan asked, using the P word knowing Lil balked at taking orders.

She nodded and strolled along the side of the barn.

Once he had a team gathered, they could look for the murder weapon and start delving into the man's background.

Chapter Four

Shandra pulled into the alley behind Ruthie's Diner.

Maxwell opened the back door of the building. His expression said it all. The sagging shoulders, downturned lips, and wrinkled brow proved he'd not had any luck talking with Ruthie.

She followed him up the stairs out of the kitchen. She'd been to Ruthie's apartment above the diner a few times over the years. The woman had been one of her first friends when she'd moved to Huckleberry.

Maxwell stood to the side in the small living room and waved to the bedroom. Shandra stepped through the bedroom door.

Ruthie was still wearing her wedding dress. Her feet were dirty. Her hose shredded up her legs. The once pristine white dress had dirt smudges. The nicely curled hair was as abstract as a pile of sticks.

Shandra sat on the edge of the bed. "Ruthie? It's me, Shandra."

Her friend opened her eyes and the sniffling turned to sobs as she reached up and grabbed Shandra around the neck, hanging on.

"Why did they come back into my life today?" she asked between sobs.

"Who? Your mother and who?" While Shandra knew the answer, she wanted to find out how and when Ruthie had seen her father.

"My mother and father. Why today and why all the lies?"

"Lies? What lies?" Shandra held Ruthie away from her. "What are you talking about and when did you see your father?"

Maxwell arrived by her side with a glass of water and a box of tissues. Ruthie took the tissue, blew her nose, grimaced when she stole a peek at Maxwell, and took the water. She sipped then shifted her attention to Shandra.

"Nearly as soon as you left with Naomi, Father stepped in the bedroom. He told me I looked beautiful and was so happy for me." She frowned. "I asked him where he'd been all these years. He said he'd realized if he stayed with mother they'd always be fighting and that wouldn't be good for me. He joined the army and sent money to her to take care of me. I called him a liar."

She spun her gaze to Maxwell. "He looked hurt and confused. He said, 'I sent your mother money and you letters.' I told him I never received any letters and mother left me at Nattie's. His face turned a dark color and anger lit up his eyes. He said he'd get to the bottom of this and stormed out of the house." She put her hand out to Maxwell. "I ruined our wedding, but I didn't know what to think, to feel. First mother shows up for the wedding, then father. And him saying he had sent money and letters… I needed to think. I ran through the woods to our place, found the keys to my car, and drove here. I just needed to think."

Shandra stood, allowing Maxwell to embrace Ruthie. The two would have to work things out. "I'll be in the other room," she said, walking into the living room.

She pulled out her phone and dialed Ryan.

"What did you find out?" he asked, not even saying hello.

"Her father approached her at my house when I left to walk up the aisle. He told her he'd sent money to her mother and letters to her. Ruthie said she never saw the letters and didn't know about the money. She said when her father left her, he was mad. She didn't know what to think, with her mother who she didn't want at the wedding and her father who she thought deserted her, both showing up. It unnerved her and she ran through the woods to their new house and drove her car here."

"I'll request Mrs. Kerby be brought in for questioning, but I still need to talk with all the other guests. Someone might have seen something when they arrived." His voice dropped. "You might stay there until I come to tell her we've found her father."

Shandra's heart ached for her friend. To finally see her father again and to learn he was dead, would be one more shock today. "Yes. I'll stay."

~*~

Ryan finished relaying what he knew to the two deputies who'd arrived. Dr. Porter, the local doctor and one of the county medical examiners, had arrived along with Mr. Treat, Maxwell's father.

"Ryan, what happened?" Mr. Treat, the local mortician, asked. "I couldn't believe when I received the call, that it was here, where we'd all gathered this afternoon for the wedding."

"I'm afraid someone didn't like the fact that Ruthie's father came to the wedding." Ryan watched the older man's face for any signs he had seen the deceased earlier.

"Donald Kerby? He was here? Neither my wife or I saw him. Was that why Ruthie changed her mind—" His eyes grew rounder. "Oh my! Does my son know about this? Have you found Ruthie?"

Dr. Porter walked back to them after having knelt by the body. "He is dead. Wasn't very long ago the blunt force trauma happened." The always professional and sometimes cold sounding doctor put a hand on Mr. Treat's shoulder. "Tell Maxwell and Ruthie, I'm sorry we missed the wedding. Mrs. Dobbins took a fall. With all your family at the wedding, I didn't have a nurse. Since Chandler was attending the wedding, Miranda assisted me."

The doctor's almost albino appearance was an opposing reflection to Mr. Treat's deep brown skin tone. Their personalities were as opposite as their appearances.

"Thank you, Dr. Porter, but they didn't get married." Mr. Treat's chin nearly touched his chest as he hung his head and swung it back and forth slightly.

Porter's gaze caught Ryan's. "Did this happen before the wedding?"

"No. Ruthie was a runaway bride." Ryan couldn't think of any other way to put it. "We found him after we had cleaned up the barn."

"I'm sure the poor girl had a good reason," Mr. Treat said. "If you're finished, I'll see that Mr. Kerby gets sent to the forensic lab in Coeur d'Alene."

"We're done." Ryan liked how fast the man came to his son's fiancée's defense. But that also made him a suspect. Had he seen Mr. Kerby and confronted him about how he'd treated Ruthie? He hadn't known her father had lived in this area his whole life.

Mr. Treat rolled the gurney past them as Ryan faced Dr. Porter.

"Could you tell anything else from the wound?"

The doctor shook his head. "Not really. It was a large object judging from the lacerations and abrasions. Either wielded by someone strong or it was heavy. The skull was cracked."

"Thank you." Ryan pivoted to give the deputies an update.

"Tell Maxwell and Ruthie, I'm sorry." He cleared his throat. "We're sorry. Still getting used to being an us," he said, his ears turning red.

"Understandable," Ryan replied. Dr. Porter and Miranda Aducci had been married by a justice of the peace in Warner a month ago. They'd decided after all that they'd been through over his aunt's death, they'd just get married and worry about his health issues when they cropped up.

Deputy Trapp walked up to him. "Gerald hasn't found any cars along the county road. This guy had to have come by ATV through the woods or someone brought him."

Ryan nodded. With no vehicle left anywhere, it was one of the two. "Call in search and rescue to comb the woods for a vehicle and possibly the weapon. From Dr. Porter's initial examination, he says it is either large and heavy or could be swung hard enough to crack a skull."

Trapp nodded. "Where are you going?"

"To tell his next of kin he's dead, see if I can get someone investigating his life the last twenty-five years, and question the people at the wedding."

Chapter Five

Shandra took a cup of tea into Ruthie.

As she set it on the bedside table, Maxwell stood. "Ruthie, why don't you get cleaned up and I'll make some dinner."

She nodded. When Shandra started to leave the room, Ruthie called her back. "What isn't Maxwell telling me?"

Shandra stood by the bed, gazing down at her friend. She looked like a doll some little girl had dragged around everywhere she went.

"Take a shower and get out of your ruined dress. The world will look better when you're cleaned up." Shandra patted her friend's shoulder and left the room, closing the door behind her.

Her phone jingled. A text from Ryan. *Be there shortly.*

She walked into the kitchen, which was larger than the living room. Maxwell was busy cutting vegetables. "Ryan's on his way."

Maxwell stabbed the knife into the cutting board.

"Why did I have to be so stupid as to drag her past, a past she wanted to forget, to her wedding?"

"You can't blame yourself. You didn't abandon her. You have been by her side for years. You've proven your love for her. Help her through this and she'll realize it even more." Shandra felt for her friends. She'd had a dysfunctional childhood and understood the anger and animosity Ruthie had. But she also understood Maxwell's actions. He'd grown up in a loving, caring family and drew his strength from that family, just as she'd learned to do since reacquainting herself with her father's family. If not for Aunt Jo, Uncle Martin, and all her cousins, she wouldn't know the strength of family. But she did, and she knew why Maxwell had asked Ruthie's mother to the wedding. He'd hoped they could start their life together with Ruthie having mended her family fences.

But who had told her father? A man that supposedly left her and her mother?

"Had you heard anyone mention knowing where Mr. Kerby was all these years?"

He shook his head. "Ruthie never mentioned him. I don't think she even cared. I didn't ask her mother when I contacted her about the wedding. I asked if there was an uncle or anyone to give Ruthie away and she said there wasn't."

"Both Ruthie's mom and dad were only children?" Shandra understood that, having grown up as an only child, but given the large families she'd witnessed in Huckleberry since moving here, she found in interesting that the Kerby's didn't have family.

"As far as I know. I could ask my dad, I think he was in school about the same time as Mr. Kerby."

She made a mental note to ask Lil as well. "What about Mrs. Kerby? Where has she been living?"

"Over in Cotton."

Shandra had made enough excursions in the area to know Cotton was a small rundown town at the far end of the county. "Does she work?"

Maxwell shrugged. "I didn't ask. I just told her about the wedding and invited her."

There was a loud knock on the building door.

"I'll get that," Maxwell said.

Shandra nodded and took stock of the food he'd laid out to discern what he'd planned to make. It appeared to be a salad. She grabbed the head of lettuce and started cleaning it up.

Maxwell and Ryan walked through the door as Ruthie stepped out of the bedroom in a T-shirt and lounge pants.

"Am I being arrested for running away from my own wedding?" she asked, her voice a bit shaky.

Ryan walked forward. "No. Ruthie." He swallowed and Shandra moved to her friend's side.

"I'm sorry to tell you, your father, Donald Kerby has been found—"

"No!" she exclaimed and started to crumple. Maxwell was by her side, scooping her up in his big arms and cradling her.

"Shhh. It's okay," he crooned, rocking her in his arms.

"Now, I'll never know," she muttered.

"Never know what?" Ryan asked.

"I'll never know if he was lying or my mother was all these years," Ruthie said. Slowly, she regained her composure and kicked her legs. "Put me down Maxwell, you big bear."

Maxwell set her feet down but kept an arm around her waist.

Ruthie wiped her face with the bottom of her shirt and stared Ryan in the eyes. "How did my father die? Was it a car wreck?"

Shandra shifted closer to Ryan. She knew while he had a job to do, he had as much affection for Ruthie as she did. They were all friends.

"I'm afraid it was a homicide."

Ruthie's eyes widened and her mouth opened in disbelief. "Some-someone killed him?"

Ryan nodded. "Behind Shandra's barn."

Her gaze riveted on Shandra. "Did you know this when you came over?"

"Yes. Ryan sent me to be with you when he came over. We knew it would be a shock."

Ruthie stepped out of Maxwell's embrace and paced the room. "Why did he come to my wedding? How did he know?" She stopped and her head whipped around, her teary eyes stared at them. "Do you think his coming to my wedding got him killed?"

"I won't have any answers for you until I research where he's been and who told him about the wedding." Ryan shifted his feet. "I have someone looking into his background now. I'll have more answers tomorrow." He shouldn't let his friendship with Ruthie skew his investigation. But he couldn't see the woman who greeted everyone in the community like family and never had a cross word for anyone other than her mother, hitting her estranged father with the anger and force of the blow the dead man had received.

"I need your mother's address and your list of wedding

guests."

Ruthie's eyes narrowed. "Maxwell knows where to find my mother. I'll get the list. It's in my bedroom."

Shandra followed Ruthie into the bedroom.

Ryan turned his attention to the big man hanging his head, a lot like his father had done earlier. "I heard you stepped out of line today."

"I thought once she saw her mother she'd forget all the resentment she had and be happy the woman was there for her wedding." He snorted. "Guess I don't know my Ruthie as well as I thought."

Ryan laughed. "It's not Ruthie, it's all women."

Treat's big goofy grin and the snap in his eyes were back. "Ain't that the truth!" He walked over to a notepad on the counter and pulled out his cell phone. "I have the address here." He glanced up, all mirth gone from his expression. "You don't think she did it, do you? I mean him coming back after all these years and all?"

"I don't know what to think. I just need to talk to all the guests at the ranch this afternoon and see if anyone saw or heard anything." Ryan knew better than to make guesses at this stage of the investigation.

Treat wrote down the address and handed it to him. He leaned close. "The house is a hovel. You might want to send someone to bring her to you."

Ryan glanced over at Treat. "She was dressed in nice clothes."

Treat grimaced. "I had my mom take her shopping for an outfit for the wedding."

"Does your mom know Mrs. Kerby?" Ryan already had the Treats on the top of his list to question from the mortician's comments.

"I don't think so. Dad met mom in college and moved her back here. All of her family live in California." Treat moved to the kitchen and started tossing chopped vegetables in a bowl. "You and Shandra want to stay for dinner?" he asked.

"Shandra can, I need to—"

"Find out what happened. I get it."

The women walked out of the bedroom.

"Here is the list," Ruthie said. She glanced at Ryan and Shandra. "When you learn more about my father, I'd really like to know where he's been all these years. Saying he left because he couldn't get along with mother and thought it would be best for me sounds lame."

"Of course, we will." Shandra put an arm around her friend.

Ryan nodded but knew she wouldn't learn a thing from him until the investigation was over. "I have to go." He glanced at Shandra.

"I'll come, too," she said, moving away from Ruthie.

"You can stay. I'm going back to work."

"No. I need to get back to the ranch." Shandra hugged her friend and patted Treat on the arm. "I'll talk to you both tomorrow."

They nodded and Ryan led Shandra down the stairs to the quiet kitchen and out the back door, making sure it pulled shut and locked.

Shandra handed him a paper. "This is the list of guests."

He took the list and put a hand on her cheek. "Don't worry. We'll figure this out."

"I know, it's just, if her father was telling her the truth, someone has been lying to her, and him, for a lot of years."

Ryan nodded. That's the part that had him thinking it was the mother. If he was paying her money and she didn't have his daughter, how did she make him think she did? And even if he was in the army, he could have checked on her or had someone check on them both. He wasn't liking the thoughts barraging his mind.

"I don't know if I'll be home tonight," he said, opening her Jeep door.

"I'm getting used to that when you're on a case. Just let me know how it's going, please?" She stepped into the Jeep and peered into his eyes.

There was little he could deny the woman. They'd set the wedding date for next June. It couldn't come soon enough for him, but Shandra wanted to have a traditional Nez Perce wedding and a Catholic wedding. She had set up for them to go to the reservation and learn the marriage dance from her aunt and cousins.

"I will let you know what I can." He kissed her briefly and shut the door.

She started up the vehicle and pulled out of the alley. The tail lights disappeared around the corner and he called dispatch. "I need Mrs. Velda Kerby, 219 Pine Road, Cotton, brought in for questioning."

Chapter Six

Shandra returned to the ranch at dark. She smiled at the warm yellow light seeping from the windows, welcoming her home. That was the best thing about having Lil for an employee. She always made sure the house was lit up and warm as if someone had been home the whole time.

Sheba ran around the side of the studio and Lil stepped out of the building as Shandra drove her Jeep up to the barn. It appeared all the law enforcement officers had left.

Before she could get out of the vehicle to open the barn doors, Lil was there, lifting the board and opening the big panels.

The lights of the Jeep revealed all the wedding decorations and accessories had been removed and stacked to the sides so she could park her vehicle in the usual spot.

"Thank you for opening the doors and finishing up the cleaning," Shandra said, sliding to the ground without being slobbered on too much by Sheba, who was happy to see her.

"Didn't take much. Ted and Naomi had to stay until the police talked to them so we kept busy." Lil walked with her to the barn doors.

"Do you have all the chores finished?" Shandra asked.

"Yep."

"Would you come in and have dinner with me? I'd like to learn more about the Kerbys." Shandra knew an invitation to a meal not cooked on her one burner hot plate would get Lil to come in for a chat.

"I can be there in two shakes of a cow's tail." Lil grasped the barn doors, swinging them shut.

"Come on in when you're ready." Shandra and Sheba entered the house through the back door.

She set out a pasta salad, a rice salad, and fried chicken. The fare for the reception had been simple food that both she and Ruthie had spent the week preparing and yesterday cooking. It was all in Shandra's refrigerator, and now freezer, until Ruthie and Maxwell picked it up.

Lil walked through the back door and turned into the laundry room. Shandra heard water running. The woman was washing her hands.

Shandra set plates and utensils for two on the counter along with a glass of wine for her and a beer for Lil.

"You're going to be eating these salads and chicken for a while," Lil said, taking the stool in front of the beer.

"I'm sure tomorrow or the next day, Maxwell or Ruthie will come take some of it off my hands." Shandra sat next to Lil and dished up the salads. "I'd like to hear everything you can think of about the Kerbys."

Lil put two drumsticks and a scoop of the pasta salad on her plate. "Don't know much more than I told you already."

"Did either of them have any brothers or sisters?" Shandra placed a chicken breast on her plate.

"Zelda didn't. She didn't have much of a family life. Her daddy was gone all the time and her mother worked a lot." Lil bit into a leg.

"And Mr. Kerby?"

"He had an older brother. Seems like he went to prison not long after Donald left."

"What was his name?" Shandra wondered at Mrs. Kerby telling Maxwell there wasn't an uncle to walk Ruthie down the aisle.

"Let me think. He would have been more my age, but I went to school over in Hafersville. The Kerbys lived toward Warner." Lil chewed some more on a chicken leg as she thought.

Shandra picked up her wine and sipped. One thing she'd discovered about Lil, if you wanted to know anything, you let her tell it in her own sweet time.

"I think the brother's name was Orin. I know he was in trouble in high school. He broke car windows and stole things during a basketball game." She stuffed a forkful of salad in her mouth.

Shandra pulled her phone from her purse and texted Ryan that Donald had a brother who'd been in trouble with the law. "What about their parents? Are they still alive?"

Lil shook her head. "They have both passed. I think before Donald left." She nodded. "Yeah, that's why Nattie took Ruthie from Zelda. There weren't any grandparents to step in and save her from her mother."

This was different. "Ruthie says her mother gave her to Nattie."

"Nope. Nattie took her away from Zelda. Told her she

wouldn't get her back until she sobered up and cleaned up." Lil shook her head. "It never happened. The woman wanted her booze and drugs more than her own daughter."

Shandra wondered if Lil was thinking of the child she'd lost so many years ago. "Was Nattie a neighbor to the Kerbys?"

"No. They lived in Warner and Nattie lived here in Huckleberry. Not sure how she came to know about Ruthie suffering at the hands of her mother."

It appeared she would need to do some investigating into Nattie as well as the Kerbys. They finished eating in silence.

When she was done, Lil slid off the stool, washed her dishes, and wandered to the back door. "See you in the morning," she called before the door clicked shut.

Shandra smiled. The woman was unique, and she was glad Lil was in her life. She cleaned up the food and her dishes with all kinds of thoughts swirling in her head. Why was Ruthie told her mother left her when the Indian woman took her? Did Donald's older brother have something to do with his disappearance? And was there enough anger in the emaciated Mrs. Kerby that she could pick up something heavy enough to kill her husband?

~*~

Ryan walked into the Huckleberry Police Station to start questioning people who had been at the wedding. He felt bad for having them dragged into the station but it was more time efficient than driving to all their houses.

The Treat family, Mr. and Mrs., Maxwell's two sisters and their husbands, and Chandler, Maxwell's brother, sat in the chairs in the waiting area.

Hazel, the seventy-something dispatcher for the

Huckleberry Police Department, had given them all something to drink. She smiled at him. "Looks like you'll be taking up space in our building again."

"Yes. Thank you for making the Treats comfortable. There will be more people showing up, please make them as comfortable as you can." He walked over to the mortician. "Mr. and Mrs. Treat, would you two follow me, please." He glanced over at the two younger couples. "Thank you for coming in. Once I finish with your mother and father, I'll speak with you." They nodded.

He walked down the hall to the one and only room used for questioning in the building. It had a three by six foot table, chairs, and boxes of records stacked along one wall. The couple entered the room. Ryan followed and closed the door.

"Thank you for coming in. I know this isn't how you planned to spend your son's wedding day."

"That didn't actually happen, now did it?" Mrs. Treat said.

"No. But, I'm sure once we discover who killed Donald Kerby, Ruthie will be ready to try again." He'd never asked what the couple thought of their son marrying Ruthie. But it appeared Mrs. Treat didn't have generous feelings toward her son's fiancée.

"Did either of you see Donald Kerby before the wedding?"

They both shook their heads.

"Did you see anyone you were curious about being there?" He studied their faces.

"Not curious, but when I took Mrs. Kerby to buy a dress, that my Maxwell paid for, I was surprised she seemed pleased for her daughter." Mrs. Treat wrinkled her nose a bit.

"Why were you surprised she was pleased?"

"She said after having a no-account for a father, she hadn't thought her Ruthie would ever stick herself to a man." Mrs. Treat sniffed. "I, of course, told her my Maxwell would never be as cowardly as the man she chose for a husband."

Ryan almost wished he'd been a fly on the wall when the two were shopping together. "You were aware that Ruthie wanted nothing to do with her mother?"

"Oh, yes! Maxwell said not to tell Ruthie. It was his surprise." Mrs. Treat rolled her eyes. "That was one thing Ruthie and I agreed on. Her mother wasn't worth her time. Who would leave their own flesh and blood for someone else to take care of and never look back? And her living so close by, she could have looked in once in a while or got herself together and took her little girl home."

He had to agree. Family was family and you didn't pass your own off on someone else. Ryan centered his gaze on Mr. Treat. "What can you tell me about Donald's older brother?"

Mr. Treat's eyes widened. "Orin? You think he killed his own brother?"

"I'm not accusing him or anyone at this point. I'm curious that when Maxwell asked Ruthie's mom about any uncles to give her away at the wedding, she said there wasn't any and I've discovered there was an uncle." Ryan noticed Mrs. Treat do one quick head shake.

"Orin was always trying to start something. He followed the goings of the Black Panther movement and thought the few other African Americans in this part of Idaho should stand up for their rights, too." Mr. Treat spread his hands. "But here, in these rural communities, we were treated just like everyone else. We didn't see a need to cause trouble for people who had accepted us."

"Is that why he went to prison?" Ryan had heard of many of the members of the BPP being thrown in jail.

"No. He worked for Mr. Narvel, driving people and things back and forth to Portland and Seattle. He was caught hauling a body in his trunk. The police said Orin killed the man and was taking him somewhere to dump him. Orin never said a word and was sent to prison."

"Do you remember when this was?" Ryan's mind was flashing through the Idaho statutes.

"It was about the time Donald left. That's all I know." Mr. Treat grasped his wife's hand. "Do you need any more from us. I'm sure Maxwell will want to talk to us."

"Actually, he and Ruthie are doing fine. They were at her apartment over the diner about an hour ago."

"Oh!" Mrs. Treat glanced at her husband. "Then she didn't run off?"

The woman seemed disappointed.

"No. She was shocked by her mother and her father showing up at her wedding and some things her father told her. She wanted to go someplace and think." Ryan stood and held out his hand. "Thank you for coming in. Would you send the other members of your family back please?"

The couple nodded as they exited the room.

Ryan texted his sister at the county office to dig up information on Orin Kerby.

Chapter Seven

Shandra wondered what Ryan was discovering as she dressed for bed and turned off the light.

Sheba lay on the bed at her feet. It was a treat for the dog when Ryan worked long hours. She was allowed to sleep on the bed and nuzzle Shandra.

"Well, girl, we had quite a day. I hope this whole thing doesn't make Ruthie skittish of marrying Maxwell." She smiled, remembering how excited Aunt Jo had been when Shandra told her she wished to learn the marriage dance. In the spring, she would go to the reservation and learn the dance from Aunt Jo. And next June, she would be married. She'd never thought about marriage but now that it was happening, she was excited to start a new adventure with Ryan.

She drifted to sleep with her hand on Sheba's large furry head.

Ella, Grandmother, appeared before Shandra. Her head moved ever so slightly as if telling her no. "No what,

Ella?" she asked. Then Maxwell and Ruthie dressed as they'd been dressed today, walked out from behind the barn. Both had splotches of red on their clothing. "They wouldn't hurt anyone. Are they going to get hurt?" Fear for her friends chilled her body. She shivered as both people dissolved before her eyes. "Ella, please tell me those two won't be hurt." She pleaded with Ella but the old Indian woman also dissolved, leaving Shandra shivering and sad.

Shandra woke from the dream feeling chilled to the bone. She got up, pulled on her warmest robe, and wandered into the kitchen to make a cup of hot cocoa. The dream played back through her mind. Were Maxwell and Ruthie in trouble? If so, why and from who?

She drifted into the living room, settling on the couch. The light on her phone blinked. She picked it up, scrolling through the screens to her text messages. A tap on Ryan's name and she texted asking him if he'd learned anything that might put the couple in danger.

Within seconds the text, *Why?* came back.

Ella came to me in a dream. Maxwell and Ruthie had blood on them and they disappeared.

As in guilty?

Her heart raced that he would even think that. *No. As dead.*

Following a lead about the deceased's brother.

OK. If you do happen to be running around, would you go by Ruthie's?

Yes.

Thank you.

Shandra set the phone down. If Ryan was looking into the brother… She pulled her laptop off the coffee table and opened it. She'd check the local papers for stories around the time Ruthie's father left. Perhaps there was more than not getting along with his wife that made him leave his family.

~*~

Ryan walked into the room he'd used to question all the guests of Maxwell and Ruthie's wedding. After five hours, he wasn't any closer to knowing how the deceased had arrived at the wedding and they were still looking for his wife, who hadn't arrived home yet. The deputy sitting on her house was now searching the Cotton bars and would work his way toward Huckleberry searching the bars as he went.

Right now, he had Nattie Small and Chea Timms in the room. The mother and daughter looked as tired and disgruntled as he felt.

"It has been a long day, Detective," Mrs. Small said.

"For everyone. I'm sorry you were the last to be questioned." Ryan took the chair across from the women. Nattie was in her seventies, her daughter, a younger version of her mother, must have been in her fifties. Both were slender, with gray in their long black braids. The daughter's demeanor more subdued, submissive.

"Have you found Ruthie? Is she well?" Mrs. Small's hands picked at the small beaded handbag on the table in front of her.

"Ruthie is above the diner. She was surprised by the appearance of her father and the things he told her." He caught Chea flinching from the corner of his eye.

"It has been too long for him to come back here and tell her he didn't mean to leave her behind." The older woman huffed and sat back in her chair, rubbing her hands

48

together. "He did not think of the poor child twenty-five years ago, why should he care today, on her wedding?"

Ryan nodded. He agreed it was strange that the man picked her wedding to come back into her life. "He told Ruthie he sent money to her mother and letters to her." There it was again the little flinch and Chea's eyes no longer studied him, they were downcast.

"If he sent money to his wife, you can be sure she would have used it for liquor and drugs. As for a letter. I have no idea." Mrs. Small leaned forward. "I saved Ruthie from a horrible life with that woman. I gave her a good home, plenty of food, and love. She is like a second daughter to me and a sister to my Chea."

He directed his attention to the younger woman. "Is that how you felt? Ruthie was a younger sister?"

She nodded but didn't make eye contact.

"If you want to know about money and letters you should talk to Zelda," Mrs. Small said, her tone indicating he was wasting his time talking with them.

He decided to take a chance on Shandra's fear of something happening to Maxwell and Ruthie. "Do you know any reason why Maxwell and Ruthie might be in danger from her father returning?"

Mrs. Small shook her head, but Chea's gaze came up to meet his, her eyes wide and fearful. He needed to talk to her alone.

Officer Blane, the young, overzealous officer who'd tried to arrest Shandra for murder when they first met, poked his head in the room. "They finally found her." Ryan nodded.

"Thank you for coming." He stood and held out his hand to shake. "Did either of you see Donald Kerby before the wedding?"

Mrs. Small scowled. "I would have given him a piece of my mind."

Chea once again cast her gaze downward.

Mrs. Small walked out of the room.

Ryan put a hand on Chea. "I have a couple of questions for you." He shut the door, detaining her.

This time she met his gaze with defiance. It seemed the woman was meek in front of her mother but not so when alone.

"Were you the one to bring Donald Kerby to the wedding?"

She didn't deny it, but also kept her lips pressed tightly.

"I'll take that as a yes. Why did he come to you?"

She continued to glare at him.

"Ok. I could tell you knew about the money and the letters. How did you know?" Nothing. "When Ruthie called him a liar, he became mad and stormed out of the house. Who was he looking for? You or his wife?"

That broke her silence. "She was no wife. She didn't care about him, the child, anything other than getting drunk or high."

That's when he realized the relationship between the deceased and this woman. "You and he were sleeping together."

Her chin came up. "Yes. He was going to leave that woman and marry me. But things happened and he had to leave." Her eyes grew wide. "But I don't know what. He said to tell me would get me killed."

"Who knew about your affair?"

"No one. Not even my mother figured it out. Donald

and I met during Ruthie's teacher conferences. We were drawn to one another. When Donald had to leave, I promised I would look after Ruthie. Telling mother about Zelda and how bright Ruthie was, it was easy to convince her that it was best for the girl to bring her to live with us." She looked away, then back. "He sent the letters to me to give to Ruthie. He didn't trust that Zelda would give them to her."

"You didn't give her the letters either." Ryan studied her. "Why didn't you give the child the connection with her father?"

"Because he said he was in trouble when he left. I didn't want his trouble to catch up to her." She bit her lip. "And I was jealous. I only received a short message to give the letters to Ruthie at school. No I miss you, how are you. There were never any return addresses for me to contact him." Her eyes narrowed. "But I learned from Zelda, when she was drunk, that Donald sent her money. I made her give me half of the money. It helped us take care of Ruthie."

Ryan peered into the woman's eyes. She told the truth. She had loved the deceased and because of that love, had helped the daughter. "You don't know what it was that sent him away?"

"No. But I think it had something to do with his brother."

A knock on the door interrupted the conversation. He answered it. "Yes."

"She's here." Blane said as the slurred yells of a distraught woman filled the station.

"Thank you. I'll take Mrs. Timms to the break room while you put my next interviewee in here."

Blane nodded, knowing the drill of putting one interviewee in the room and then escorting Mrs. Timms out to the waiting room.

Ryan opened the door and motioned for the woman to walk ahead of him down the hall farther into the building. "From the sounds of Mrs. Kerby, it would be best if she didn't see you."

The woman nodded and stood in the break room.

"I'll have Officer Blane escort you out when I get in the room with Mrs. Kerby." He put a hand on the woman's arm. "Thank you for being honest with me. It's the only way we can find justice for Donald and his daughter."

She nodded.

Ryan poured two cups of coffee and strode back down the hall. He glanced at the big clock in the main area. Two in the morning. No wonder he felt bone tired. But he couldn't take a break until he had this discussion with Mrs. Kerby.

He tapped on the door with a knuckle.

Blane opened the door, allowing him entry. Ryan placed one of the cups of coffee on the table in front of the drunk woman.

"I could use a cup, thought maybe you could, too," he said by way of starting the conversation.

He felt Blane slip out of the room.

"Why did you drag me into a police station? I ain't done nothin' to no one." Mrs. Kerby looked at the coffee but pushed it to the middle of the table.

"Mrs. Kerby, do you know why we brought you in?" It was apparent she was close to the toxic stage of being drunk. Her eyes couldn't focus, her actions jerky, and her words slurred.

"No. Some policeman pulled me out of my favorite bar and drove me here." She laid her head down on the table. "I just want to go home and go to bed."

"Mrs. Kerby, do you have anywhere in Huckleberry you could spend the night? We could continue this discussion in the morning."

Tears rolled down the woman's cheeks. "I don't have no one. My daughter didn't even want to see me on her wedding day." Sobs shook her dried-up body.

It was clear he wasn't going to have a beneficial conversation with her. "How about we put you up in a motel for the night and talk with you in the morning?"

He didn't want to upset her more with the news of her husband tonight. He wasn't sure what she would do. He wanted her sober when he asked her several pointed questions.

Her sobs abated and she raised her head. "You'd do that? You'd put me in a motel for the night?"

He nodded. "Would that be okay with you?"

She nodded.

"I'll make the arrangements."

Chapter Eight

Shandra had glanced at the clock when Ryan slipped into bed. Three-thirty.

She crept out of the room at seven to make breakfast and wait for him to wake. Mornings after his late nights he usually was up by eight and headed out by eight-thirty. She wanted to have breakfast ready for him so she would have time to ask him about his questioning.

Sleep had been long coming after the dream the night before. It had taken all of her control to not pick up the phone and call Ruthie, just to make sure her friend was okay.

When her grandmother first came to her in dreams she'd thought she'd gone crazy. With Ryan believing in the dreams and the clues Ella gave her helping them solve murders the last couple of years, she now believed and viewed them as a way to help Ryan.

Which was why she planned to hang out with Ruthie today.

Right on cue, Ryan walked into the kitchen dressed and ready for work. "Something smells good in here." He kissed her cheek and picked up the plate piled with hot cakes, eggs, and bacon. "I missed dinner last night."

She filled a cup with coffee for him and took her tea over to the stool next to where he sat. "Long day."

"Yeah."

"Did you learn anything helpful?" She sipped her tea, watching him over the rim.

"Not really."

She could tell by the way he didn't look at her, he knew something he didn't want to tell her. So, he had learned something. He didn't keep information from her unless he thought doing so would keep her safe.

"Is this more than a crime of passion?" she asked.

His gaze latched onto hers. "Why do you ask?"

"If it was a crime of passion, you would be telling me what you learned."

His eyebrow rose as he studied her. "What makes you think I learned something?"

She laughed. "We've been together long enough and through some tough times. I can tell when you aren't telling me something, thinking it's for my own good."

He sighed. "I should have known you'd see through me." Ryan drank his coffee and picked up a piece of bacon. "I'm not sure if what I learned is harmful to you, but I don't want you telling Ruthie. If she knew what I learned last night, she might muck things up."

This intrigued her. What could he have learned that would upset Ruthie? "You're withholding this information from me to make sure she doesn't find out about it?"

"Yes." He leaned over and kissed her cheek. "I know

you can be trusted, but she is a good friend and you may feel compelled to help her."

Shandra nodded. He knew her too well. "But you *will* tell me what you learned?"

"When it won't hinder my investigation." He stood. "Got to go. They pulled Mrs. Kerby in last night and she was so drunk I couldn't tell her about her husband, let alone question her. We put her up in a motel in Huckleberry overnight."

Shandra stood. "I'm going to check on Ruthie this morning."

Ryan put a hand on her arm. "I don't think she knows why her father is back or why he left. Don't go poking around for information."

Her face heated. She'd been poking around on the internet last night and had come up with information about the uncle.

"What have you found?" His gaze became intent.

"I searched the local newspaper archives for nineteen-seventy to nineteen-seventy-four. There was a brief story about Orin Kerby being found with a body in his car. He worked for a corporation that I'm pretty sure I discovered while checking out Mrs. Narvel's husband."

Ryan held up his hand. "Stop. I have police checking all of this out. Don't go near anyone who worked for Narvel or this corporation or bring it up to Ruthie. All I need is the three of you nosing around where you shouldn't be."

"Three of us?"

"You know wherever you and Ruthie go, Maxwell will be right with you."

She smiled. That was true. He wouldn't let them dig

around without him.

He grasped her chin. "Promise me."

The concern and warmth in his eyes made her heart smile. "I promise to not dig into Mr. Kerby's past. And I won't say a thing to Ruthie."

"Good." He kissed her on the lips and backed away. "I'll let you know if I'll be home late."

She nodded. If anyone had told her three years ago she'd be engaged right now and looking forward to marriage, she would have told them they were delusional. But she could hardly wait for June.

~*~

Ryan walked into the Huckleberry Police Station, expecting to see the daytime dispatcher, Millie, instead, Hazel sat behind the desk her eyes barely open.

"Where's Millie?" he asked.

"She's under the weather. Called in sick." Hazel waved her hand. "I'm too old to pull two shifts."

"I agree. I'll talk to Chief Sandberg." He strode toward the hallway.

"Mrs. Kerby is in the interview room."

"Thanks."

Ryan entered the chief's office. The big man with a Nordic ancestry sat behind his desk a pair of small reading glasses perched on the end of his nose. He glanced up. "Detective Greer. What can I do for you? Sounds like you picked up another homicide at your fiancée's."

It had become a bit of joke around this station and the county office that he was marrying Shandra because she kept him busy with murder investigations.

"Yes, I have another homicide. Any chance you could send Hazel home? She was here all night and won't do us any good if she falls asleep."

Sandberg set his glasses on the desk. "I would if I had someone to take her place. With this investigation, we have deputies in and out, calling here, and our two officers helping out as well as doing their duties. We need a dispatcher."

"Maybe you need to find someone to come in and learn the ropes so you can call them in when you need a third dispatcher." He had wondered at the efficiency of this station from the first time he'd worked with them. It was a small force that was spread thin. Hazel was a volunteer.

"I'll make some phone calls." Chief Sandberg put his glasses back on his nose and glanced down at the papers on his desk.

Ryan understood he had been dismissed.

He backtracked to the interview room.

Mrs. Kerby's upper body sprawled across the table. A soft snore was the only sound in the room. Whoever brought her in, must have picked her up and carried her. She still wore the nice pants suit she'd worn yesterday. Only now it wasn't as pristine.

He left the room, walked to the break room, filled two heavy paper cups with coffee, and returned to the interview room. With a grip on the hot cups, he kicked the leg of the chair the woman sat in.

"Mrs. Kerby? Mrs. Kerby, I have coffee." He gave the chair another kick.

The snoring stopped and she rubbed a hand over her face.

"Mrs. Kerby. This is Detective Greer. I have coffee for you," he said louder.

"Huh?" She shoved a hand over her face again as if the

motion would make things work and wake her up.

He placed the cups on the table as far away from the woman as he could set them and grasped her shoulder, giving her a good shake. "Mrs. Kerby. You're in the police station. I have information for you."

"What? Information?" her eyes opened tentatively and slammed back down. "Go away!"

"I'm sorry. I can't. I need to talk with you. It's important."

She slowly pushed with her hands, righting her body and leaning back in the chair. With the same measured steps, her eyelids raised. The dark brown irises masked the pinpoint pupils. "Where am I?"

Ryan sighed and started over. "We brought you in to the Huckleberry PD last night. You weren't in any condition to talk with. We put you up in a motel. An officer brought you here this morning." He handed her a coffee cup.

She sipped and winced. "Why did you need to bring me to a police station?"

"I have some bad news—"

"Ruthie? What happened to Ruthie?" The woman slopped coffee over her hand and the table when she slammed the cup down.

"Ruthie is fine. It's your husband."

"Donald? I haven't seen him in over twenty years." She picked the cup back up, ignoring the light brown liquid sliding down her hand.

"He was at the wedding yesterday."

"No, he wasn't. I didn't see him." Her eyes widened and fear emanated from their depths.

"He was. He talked with Ruthie."

"No!" she yelled. "He wasn't supposed to come back. Ever. He told me if he came back he'd be a dead man. He said to keep us safe, he would stay away."

"What was he afraid of?" Ryan latched onto the ominous threat that kept popping up.

She shook her head. "I don't know. He said if he told me, I'd also be in trouble like he was. He said leaving was the best thing he could do for the people he loved."

"And he sent you money?"

Her head jerked and her eyes narrowed. "Who said he sent money?"

"He told Ruthie he sent her money." Ryan could see the woman trying to figure out what to say.

"He told Ruthie? Shit!" She ran a hand over her short dreadlocks and stared at a spot on the wall over his shoulder.

"Why didn't you tell Ruthie about the money? Why didn't you give her his address to write to him?"

"I didn't want her writin' him back and tellin' him she was took from me. He would have stopped sending money." She glanced up. "Nattie give her a better life than I could. I've got an addiction I can't shake." Her mind seemed to finally catch up with the conversation. "Is he here? In Huckleberry?"

"No. He was murdered yesterday behind Shandra's barn. Sometime after the wedding disbanded." He was still waiting for the report from forensics.

"Murdered? As in dead?" Her face drooped and her saggy jowls jiggled a bit.

"Yes. Can you think of anyone who was at the wedding who would want him dead, besides you?"

"Me!" She shoved back in the chair. "Why would I

want him dead?"

"He left you and your daughter."

"But he sent money. I didn't care he was gone. Less work cooking and cleaning."

He believed her. She wasn't the domestic type. Or the mother type. "Can you think of anyone else there who would be angry enough to kill him?"

Her eyes widened, then she shuttered them and shook her head. She'd thought of someone. Who?

"You're sure?"

She nodded and took a sip of her coffee.

"Where did he work before he left?"

"Odd jobs. Gas station. Helped some putting in the ski resort."

He decided to change tactics. "Why didn't you tell Maxwell about Ruthie's Uncle Orin?"

"He's in prison. She doesn't even know she has an uncle. That's the one thing Nattie and I agreed on. Not telling her about Orin."

"Why?" He was beginning to think poor Ruthie had been lied to her whole life.

"Because her daddy ran off and her uncle was in prison. We didn't want her dwelling on the fact she could have bad blood in her." The woman stared at him as if this was a scientific fact.

He shook his head. "A good stable environment, like she had, is all a child needs to grow up to be a good person. And even some of those go bad. It isn't in the blood."

The woman stared at him as if he didn't know what he was talking about.

"Did Orin also work building the ski resort?"

She nodded. "He drove the architects and bigwigs

around. Orin never did anything that got his hands dirty. He said, we weren't slaves anymore and shouldn't have to do manual labor."

"But your husband did?"

"Yeah. Donald did anything that brought in money. He was a laborer which didn't set well with Orin. The two of them got into arguments all the time. The last one was the night Orin was arrested. Donald left several days after that."

Ryan jotted this information down in his notebook. "Do you think Donald knew something about the body found in Orin's car?"

Her face paled. "I hope not. Orin killed that man. That would make the daddy of my child a murderer."

"Any idea how the man was involved with Orin or your husband?"

"I never heard of the man when I read about it." She finished off the coffee. "Can I see Donald?"

"His body is in Coeur d'Alene determining cause of death."

"You said it was murder?"

"We're trying to determine what the murder weapon was." He stood. "Thank you for coming in. I'm sure Treat and Son Mortuary will contact you when the body comes back."

She nodded but didn't stand. "Do you mind if I sit here a spell?"

"I'll give you ten minutes and an officer will take you home." Ryan walked out of the room and straight to the desk and computer he'd been given when working cases in Huckleberry. He logged in and checked his emails for the reports on Orin Kerby's arrest.

Chapter Nine

Shandra wasn't surprised to see Ruthie's Diner open for business. The woman was supposed to be on her honeymoon and the place closed down for five days. But Ruthie didn't know the word relax. And knowing her father was killed the day before, Shandra was pretty sure her friend needed the work to not think about all the years she'd missed with the man.

It appeared the diner regulars had come to find out what had happened to cause their favorite cook to be at work and not on her honeymoon. Or they'd heard about the death and were curious how Ruthie was holding up.

Every booth was full, and all but one stool at the counter. Shandra grabbed the stool as Ruthie looked through the window from the kitchen to the seating. She waved a spatula.

The young waitress, Trudy, placed a glass of water in front of her and a menu.

"Where's Maxwell?" she asked the waitress.

"He's in the back prepping. They were lucky to catch me or they'd be serving this crowd by themselves. Ruthie gave everyone five days off." Trudy hurried over to take an order from a booth of senior citizens. All locals, no doubt, here to learn the gossip on the non-wedding.

"Your usual?" Ruthie asked, stepping out of the kitchen for a moment and filling a large cup with soda.

"If you have the time and energy. This is some crowd for a restaurant that is supposed to be closed." She eyed her friend.

"I couldn't sit around doing nothing for four days." Her voice lowered. "Has Ryan learned anything about who killed my father?"

Shandra shook her head. "He questioned all the guests last night and was talking to your mom this morning."

Ruthie shrugged that off. "Nattie called me this morning to see how I was. She also asked me what my father had said to me."

The uncertainty on her friend's face brought out Shandra's protectiveness. "What did you tell her?"

"Everything. I have no reason to think Nattie killed my father. She had harsh words for him over the years, but not the outright hatred that it would take to kill—" She spun and headed into the kitchen.

Shandra slid off the stool and followed. She put her arms around her friend.

"I should have hugged him and been thankful he came instead of accusing him of being a liar. Maybe if I had he'd still…"

"You couldn't have known someone else was angrier with him than you." Shandra comforted her friend.

Maxwell came from the back of the kitchen. He took

over holding Ruthie. "I told her we didn't have to open up. We could hide out or still go on our trip. But she didn't want to leave without knowing what happened to her father." He tipped his head toward the grill. "And she likes to cook when she's upset."

Ruthie flew out of his arms and flipped burgers and juggled baskets of fries.

"You want me to help? I'm between projects right now." Shandra walked over to a white apron hanging on a hook.

"We can use you back here. I gave everyone the week off thinking we'd be closed," Ruthie said.

Shandra ducked her head into the apron and tied the back. "Give me orders." This was the best way to stay close to the two and hopefully pick up on the gossip about the murder. It was a small town. Locals talked and locals knew the history better than she did.

She washed the dishes and helped make fresh salads. By the time the lunch crowd had left, her stomach was growling. Ruthie handed her a basket with her favorite burger and sweet potato fries.

"Let's eat." Ruthie and Maxwell followed her out to the eating area. They all sat at a booth and dug into the burgers.

Trudy brought over three cups and poured iced tea into them.

"Thank you," Shandra said, taking a sip.

Ruthie stared at her over her raised burger. "What have you found out?"

Shandra bit into her burger to give her time to consider what to say. Ryan had told her not to tell Ruthie what he'd discovered, but he'd not said anything about her telling what she'd learned. Would telling her friend about an uncle she didn't know she had hurt the investigation? She didn't think so.

"Ryan told me I couldn't tell you anything until he had more facts."

Ruthie nodded. "I didn't ask what Ryan had discovered. I asked what you have." Ruthie gave her an "I know you are digging into this" look.

"Come on, Shandra. We know you won't stay out of this. Another body on your ranch and your friend's father…" Maxwell shook a french fry at her.

She sighed. "You two know me too well." She eyed her friend. "You have an uncle. Your father's brother."

Ruthie leaned back. "No? Really? An uncle?" She glanced at Maxwell.

By his downcast eyes and darker color on the tips of his ears, he knew.

Ruthie slapped his arm. "You knew and didn't tell me?"

He shrugged. "When you said you didn't have any relatives and your mother told me the same thing, when my dad said he was sure that your dad had a brother, I looked into it."

"Why didn't you tell me?" Ruthie tossed her burger in her basket and stared at Maxwell as she wiped her fingers on a napkin.

"When I discovered he went to jail for killing a man and your mom obviously didn't want you to know, I thought I'd leave it be." He shrugged and kissed her cheek. "It was because I love you."

She leaned away from him. "If you loved me you wouldn't keep any secrets."

"He's only trying to keep you safe," Shandra said.

"Safe from what? My dysfunctional family? I won't fall apart discovering I have an uncle in prison." Ruthie threw her hands in the air. "Why does everyone think I'll fall apart?" Her eyes widened. She stared first at Shandra, then Maxwell. "Do you think I'll hit the bottle or take drugs like my mother? I'm not that weak."

"I would never call you weak. And no, I don't think you would become your mother. I just don't want to upset your relationship with this great guy sitting next to you. Now that I've found a man I can trust, I want my friends to enjoy the same thing." Shandra meant every word. Ruthie was one of the strongest women she'd ever met and she deserved the love Maxwell had for her.

"I know you are too strong to become like your mother. There must have been something that caused your father to leave you behind when he left." Maxwell grasped Ruthie's hand. "And his strength is what I see in you. And love about you."

Ruthie's eyes softened as she gazed into his.

Shandra became uncomfortable witnessing the exchange. She bit into her burger and let the two communicate with their eyes.

The door opened and they all glanced over.

Shandra's heart skipped a beat and she smiled.

Ryan strode over to the table and plopped down beside her. "I heard you had opened up today," he said, plucking a fry from Shandra's basket.

"She couldn't stay still," Maxwell offered.

"Can you tell me anything?" Ruthie asked.

Ryan stared into the woman's eyes and wished he could tell her what he knew, but for now it was best to keep it all to himself and his reports. He shook his head slowly and picked up another fry. "I'm sorry. What I've learned so far has to stay in the reports. I'm still waiting for the forensic report." His phone vibrated.

He pulled it out. Forensics. "Excuse me." He slid out of the booth and walked out onto the street.

"Greer."

"Sheila Rickman," said the female voice on the other end. "I sent an email with the full report to you, but thought you might like to know the victim was hit from behind with, according to the fragments I dug out of the abrasions, a wood object."

"Wood? Is that heavy enough to have caused that much damage if a woman swung it?" He couldn't see Mrs. Kerby or Chea or even Nattie swinging a hunk of wood and causing the damage he'd seen.

"If it was long enough and they were angry enough. The weight of the object would have caused more momentum on impact if it had been long. There were several posts and limbs found in the area that were brought in for testing. I'll let you know if one of those is the weapon."

"Thank you." He shoved his phone into the holster on his belt and walked back into the diner. The three at the booth had their heads together talking quietly.

"Any chance I can get a burger?" he asked, returning to his spot beside Shandra.

"Coming right up." Ruthie slid out of the booth and headed for the kitchen.

"Did your call have to do with the case?" Shandra asked.

"Yes. And I'm not telling you what it is. You are in

cahoots with people involved in the case." He picked up another sweet potato fry. He didn't normally eat them but he was hungry.

"What do you mean involved?" Treat asked him.

"The victim is the father of your fiancée. I'm not at liberty to tell you or Ruthie, or you—" he glanced pointedly at Shandra, "—what I find out on the case. You'll all have to wait like everyone else."

Treat nodded, but Shandra's brows knit together as if she were deep in thought.

Ruthie returned with a burger and fries and the waitress followed behind with a tall glass of iced tea.

"Thank you," he said to both women and picked up the burger. He glanced up to find three pairs of eyes watching him. The food stuck in his throat. A drink of tea helped to wash some of it down.

"Is there anything you can tell me about my dad?" Ruthie asked.

"He wasn't lying about joining the army." He took another bite and chewed.

"Why would he do that?" Ruthie said, glancing at both Treat and then Shandra. The two both shrugged.

"Do you know where? What group he was in? Maybe I can find someone to talk to and learn more about him." Ruthie's eyes brightened with the idea.

"I'm not sure that's a good idea. For all we know someone from his time in the army followed him here." He decided to change the conversation to help him. "Chea Timms told me she was your teacher in grade school. That she was the one that convinced her mother you should live with them. Did Chea marry? She has a different name than her mother."

Ruthie nodded. "She was my teacher, and she was always nice to me. I thought that was why mother gave me to Nattie, because I was always talking about Miss Small. Chea married probably seven or eight years after I moved in with them. Her husband is different but nice. He's also a teacher."

"He wasn't at the wedding," Ryan said, just now realizing it.

She frowned. "I didn't know that." Her face flushed. "I didn't see who had come. I ran out of the house in the opposite direction of the barn."

Treat put his hand over hers. "It's okay. We'll go to the justice of the peace next week."

She nodded.

"No wedding?" Shandra asked.

"No. We decided that we don't need all of that. We'll just get the papers signed next week and be done with all the formalities." Treat smiled at Ruthie.

"I think that's a good idea considering everything that happened at the first attempt," Shandra said.

Ryan studied Shandra. Would she rather do that than the traditional ceremony with the Nez Perce and the Catholic ceremony his mother expected?

"Why did you ask about Chea's husband?" Shandra asked.

"Just curious. He never came up in the conversation I had with Chea and Mrs. Small." Ryan tried to convey to Shandra to drop it.

"Did you really question everyone who was at the wedding?" Ruthie asked.

"Yes. But no one saw your father or anyone who didn't belong there." Ryan shoved some fries in his mouth.

"Why did your father make the effort to come see you but not want anyone to see him?" Shandra asked.

"Someone did," Treat said solemnly.

Ruthie nodded, tears glinting in her eyes.

"Just go about your business and try not to think about it." Ryan knew that was asking too much of all three.

"When will we be able to bury him?" Ruthie asked.

"Soon. When forensics is done, they'll send him to the mortuary." He glanced at Treat.

He nodded. "We'll let you know and we can make arrangements."

Ruthie's lips quivered. She rose, taking the empty baskets and hurrying into the kitchen.

"She's not taking any of this well. That her father made the attempt to see her on her wedding has her rethinking the anger she's had toward him." Treat stood. "Tough one knowing your father may have died trying to see you."

Ryan nodded.

Treat picked up their glasses and wandered into the kitchen.

Ryan motioned to the white apron on Shandra. "They pull you in to wash dishes?"

She smiled. "I came to check on Ruthie and found them with a packed diner and offered to help since Ruthie had given everyone the week off. She was lucky to call in Trudy."

"Will you be home later?" he asked.

"Yeah. I'll help with the dinner crowd and head home." She raised an eyebrow. "Will you be there?"

"Unless something comes up."

Her smile spread and her eyes lit up. "Good. Sheba is

fluffy and comforting, but you make me feel safer when I have my dreams."

"Is that the only reason you keep me around?" he asked.

"One of many reasons."

He kissed her on the lips and slid out of the booth. "See you tonight." Ryan strode to the door and glanced into the kitchen. Treat had Ruthie in his arms, comforting her. He had to find out who killed her father. Not only to give her closure, but to make sure everyone in the community was safe.

Chapter Ten

Shandra finished washing the dishes and picked up the large black bag of trash to take out to the big metal bin in the alley behind the building. Ruthie had told her to go home two hours ago but the people kept pouring into the diner. She would have bet every local had been in today.

She opened the back door and kicked something that scratched across the pavement. Another step sent the object scratching across the pavement again. A step to the side, and she walked over, dumped the garbage in the bin, and glanced at the ground.

An old shoe box sat on the pavement. She picked it up, carrying it into the light of the kitchen.

"Whatcha got?" Maxwell asked.

"I don't know. It was in front of the door and I kicked it when I walked out." She lifted the lid and discovered letters addressed to Ruthie. Raising her gaze to Maxwell's she said, "I think these are the letters Ruthie's father talked about."

Maxwell was by her side in two strides. He peered down into the box. "Call Ryan and tell him." He took the box and set it on the prep table. "I'll go get Ruthie."

Shandra pulled out her phone and hit the number one button.

"You aren't home," Ryan answered.

She smiled. "You must be. I just took the trash out and was headed that way when I found a shoe box."

"What was in it?" His tone was all seriousness.

"It looks like the letters sent by Ruthie's father. They have her name on the envelopes. That's all."

"It appears my questioning jogged a guilty conscience."

Shandra drew in a breath. "You know who had them. Was it her mother?"

"It's all part of the investigation. But if there is anything in those letters that says why her father left, I need to know." There was the cop she'd first met.

"I may be a little later."

"I'll make something that will hold over."

The phone went silent as Maxwell led Ruthie to the back of the kitchen.

"These were sitting in front of the door," Shandra said, motioning to the box.

Ruthie walked forward and stared down into the box. "The letters!" She picked one up and turned it over and over. "Where? How?"

"Ryan said he must have jogged someone's conscience when questioning people."

"My mother?" Ruthie asked.

"I don't know. He wouldn't say." Shandra picked an envelope up. "He said, if your father mentions why he left, to let him know."

She nodded and opened the letter in her hand. Tears trickled down her cheeks as she read and passed it over to Maxwell. He read it and placed it on the table. They did that with each one, until there was a pile of papers and a pile of envelopes.

"He doesn't say anything about why he left, only that he did it for mother's and my safety. He doesn't even tell me what he's doing. Only that he loves me and hopes to see me again someday." Ruthie tapped the stack of letters. "What did he do that he felt he had to leave so mother and I were safe?"

Shandra shrugged. "That could be what caused his death. The person he was hiding from must have discovered he came back for your wedding and wanted to make sure he kept quiet."

"What could he have seen?" Maxwell asked.

"Do you remember who he worked for?" Shandra took off her apron.

Ruthie shook her head. "I was so small, I didn't care about that. I just knew I enjoyed being with him when he was home."

"I'll ask my dad. He should remember," Maxwell said.

"Ryan's making me dinner. I better get home." She hugged Ruthie. "Do you want me to come help again tomorrow?"

"I think most of the community has discovered Maxwell and I are still together even though there wasn't a wedding. I think things will be quiet now. There's no need for you to come to town."

"I'll check in anyway. Good night." Shandra picked up her purse and jacket hanging by the back door and walked out into the night. She strolled down the alley and turned the corner to walk to where she'd parked her Jeep on the side street that morning.

She climbed into the vehicle, clicked the seat belt, and started the engine. Before she turned on her lights, she spotted a vehicle in her rearview mirror. The small dark car drove into the alley behind the diner. Why would a car drive down the alley? Maybe they were going to the back of the apartments at the other end.

A twist of the key and the Jeep started up. She pulled away from the curb and onto Huckleberry Street. A glance in her mirror caused her to slam on the brakes. The light pouring into the street on the block of Ruthie's restaurant didn't look right. She reversed and discovered flames lapping at the inside of Ruthie's Diner.

She dialed 911. "There's a fire at Ruthie's Diner!" she said, before bailing out of the vehicle and running for the front door.

"Ruthie! Maxwell!" she screamed. Just as she reached for the door, it slammed open. Maxwell lunged out, holding Ruthie in his arms.

"Thank God!" Shandra said, leading them to the middle of the street.

Sirens whined through the still night air. People started lining up on the street as the fire truck arrived.

EMTs rushed over to them, putting an oxygen mask on Ruthie and arguing with Maxwell to get him to put one on.

When Chief Sandberg strode up to the fire chief, Shandra left her friends in the care of the EMTs.

"Chief Sandberg, I'm Shandra Higheagle. I was leaving the diner when I saw a car drive into the alley."

The tall, broad shouldered man had white hair and

strong facial features. His piercing green eyes studied her. "Can you describe the vehicle?"

"I didn't pay that much attention. It was a sedan. Dark colored. I thought it was strange it drove down the alley but other than that I didn't realize I would need to know the license plate." She'd let her friend down. Thinking on it now, she should have questioned the vehicle driving down the alley and backed up to get the plate and she might have seen them commit arson. She glanced over at Maxwell and Ruthie. They could have been killed.

People started gathering.

"I'll have someone check out your allegations of arson." The chief strode over to a deputy sheriff who'd pulled up.

She nodded and walked over to Ruthie and Maxwell. The EMTs had removed the oxygen mask from Ruthie. "Let me take you home," Shandra said, putting a hand on her friend's shoulder.

Ruthie appeared to be in shock as she stared at the rock building going up in smoke.

Maxwell nodded. "Don't know if our car is burned or not but I don't want to stick around here." He tugged on Ruthie's hand. "Come on. Let's go home."

Ruthie shook her head. "My diner…my apartment."

"You both got out with your lives. Insurance and community will help you rebuild," Shandra said, putting an arm around Ruthie's shoulders. "Come on."

Deputy Trapp approached them. "Shandra, Miss Kerby, Maxwell." The man nodded to each of them. "I need to take your statements. If this was arson as Shandra indicated to the chief, we need to know what went on."

Shandra glanced at her friend. She wasn't in any shape

to answer questions. "Could you follow us to their house? She needs to get away from this sight."

The deputy nodded. "I'll follow you."

"Thank you." Shandra smiled. If the people who started the fire wanted Ruthie and Maxwell dead, they might try again if they saw the two still alive.

Once Maxwell and Ruthie were in her back seat, holding onto one another, Shandra dialed Ryan.

"Haven't you left yet?" he asked.

"Leaving now. But there's been a change of plans. Someone set the diner on fire with Maxwell and Ruthie in it. They're both fine. I'm driving them to their house on the county road. Deputy Trapp is following to get our statements."

"I'll be there waiting for you."

"Thank you!" She tapped the off button, smiling. Ryan always knew when she needed his support.

Behind the wheel of her Jeep, she started the engine and headed out of the town. The bobbing lights behind her gave a feeling of security. Maxwell and Ruthie said nothing all the way to their house. It was about thirty-five minutes from town and ten minutes from her house.

Ryan sat in his pickup in the driveway as she drove up.

"What's Ryan doing here?" Maxwell asked.

"I called to tell him I would be late and he offered to come over."

"I'm glad he's here," Ruthie said. "I want to ask him about the letters."

"Oh no! Did they get burned up in the fire?" Shandra asked, turning off the engine.

"Nope. I had just tucked them into my coat pocket when something crashed through the back window and the kitchen became full of flames." Maxwell patted his pocket.

"I'm glad those were saved." Shandra's door opened and Ryan lifted her out.

"Were you in the diner when it caught fire?" The concern and anger on his face took all her other worries away.

"No. But I think I saw the car the arsonists were driving."

Deputy Trapp walked up. "Greer. Didn't expect to see you here."

Ryan spun toward his co-worker. "I didn't expect to see you either." He wasn't going to say any more. But ever since Shandra called, he had a feeling the fire had something to do with Donald Kerby's murder.

"I'm here to take statements." He nodded to Shandra. "Your fiancée suggested I do it here."

They all walked into the newly remodeled house. Knowing Ruthie and Maxwell as well as he did, he would have known it was their house without being told. There was a mix of Native American influence, African American, and bright colors. There wasn't a boring area in the living room or dining room, the rooms seen as he walked into the house.

"I'll make coffee and hot water," Shandra said, hurrying into the kitchen.

Ryan was torn between helping Shandra just to be near her and know she was okay, and hearing what Maxwell and Ruthie had to say.

He sat down on a chair to the side of the couch where Maxwell and Ruthie collapsed. Trapp stood in front of them.

"Take a load off," Ryan said to the deputy.

Trapp frowned but took the hint and pulled a dining room chair over to sit across the coffee table from the distraught couple. "Tell me what you were doing and what happened."

Maxwell started. "We were finishing up the cleaning to go home. Shandra had walked out the back door not five minutes before we heard the back window break. Before I had time to see the cause, smoke filled the room. Ruthie was grabbing her cookbooks when I pulled her out of the kitchen. She collapsed from the smoke and I carried her outside."

Ryan's gut clenched at the mention Shandra had only been out of the building less than five minutes. Had she seen the people who did it? Was that why she wanted him here?

The woman in his thoughts walked into the room with cups of coffee and tea. She handed the first cup of tea to Ruthie, then passed the coffees to the men. Shandra picked up the other cup of tea and sat down beside her friend.

"Miss Kerby, did you see or hear anything other than what Maxwell stated?" Trapp asked.

Ruthie shook her head.

Trapp shifted his attention to Shandra. "What did you see?"

Ryan leaned forward. He wanted to hear everything she had to say.

"I left the diner through the back door. Walked down the alley to the street. Got in my Jeep and looked in the rearview mirror. That's when I saw a sedan turn into the alley. I wondered who it could be, then started my car and drove to Huckleberry street. I turned to head home and saw the flash of light in my mirror. I backed up and was headed into the diner through the front door when Maxwell carried Ruthie out."

Ryan's head throbbed. She would have charged into the burning building after her friends.

"Do you have any more of a description of the vehicle you saw go into the alley?" Trapp asked.

Shandra shook her head. "I didn't realize it was anything important when I spotted it. Just a dark sedan."

Trapp closed his book, gulped the coffee, and stood. "If you think of anything else you can tell Detective Greer."

Ryan stood, following Trapp to the door. "What do you know about this?"

"The same as you. What those three people in there told me and that it was arson. The accelerant was found in the back of the kitchen about ten feet from the broken window." He opened the door and stepped out into the night. "You don't think this has anything to do with the homicide you're working, do you?"

"I hope not, but that woman is the daughter of the victim. She hadn't seen him in close to twenty-five years and now that he's surfaced, he's dead and her diner was torched." Ryan shook his head. "I don't like the coincidence."

Chapter Eleven

Shandra glanced up when Ryan closed the door and wandered over to her side.

"What's that?" he asked, pointing to the letters Maxwell had piled on the coffee table.

"The letters my father wrote to me," Ruthie said, her fingers fluttering the pages.

Ryan dropped to his knees beside the table. "It's good you were able to save them. When did these show up at the restaurant?" he directed his question to Shandra.

"Ten minutes before I left?" she said, peering at both Maxwell and Ruthie.

"I'd say closer to fifteen or twenty minutes," Maxwell said. "You brought them in, called Ryan, then we read them, and had finished cleaning up when you left."

"That's true," Shandra agreed. "Why?" She studied Ryan's face.

"And did you read anything that might tell us why your father left?" He was watching Ruthie.

"I didn't see anything. Did you Maxwell?" Ruthie's red-rimmed gaze landed on the man next to her.

"He mostly just said he missed Ruthie and wished he could visit, but he didn't want to put her and her mother in danger."

"Nothing about where he was or what he was doing?" Ryan picked up several sheets, scanning them.

"No." Maxwell said, also picking up sheets and reading them.

"What was the return address?" Ryan asked.

"There wasn't one. Just Ruthie's name on the envelope," Shandra said.

Ryan's head whipped around and he stared at her. "Just her name?"

"Y-yes. Why?"

"She knows more." Ryan stood.

"Who knows more?" Shandra followed him to his feet.

He tossed a glance toward Ruthie. "I need to go." He grasped Shandra's hand, pulling her toward the door. They both stepped outside.

"You go home and stay there," he said. "I don't like that someone knew about the letters and thought there might be information in them that needed to be burned along with anyone who might have read them."

"The person who had the letters? Why hasn't she been harmed?" Shandra wanted to know who it was but had a hunch it was Ruthie's mother.

"I don't know. Unless they didn't know about the letters until now, when Donald Kerby returned and mentioned them to his daughter." He kissed her quick. "I have to go. Go home. I'll be there as soon as I talk to someone."

Shandra watched him jog to his vehicle and tear out of the driveway. She spun around and found Maxwell sitting on the couch by himself, reading the letters.

He glanced up. "Ruthie went in to take a shower."

She nodded. "I'm going to go. Tell her I'll check in tomorrow." A thought came to her. "How much damage do you think there was to the diner?"

"I'm not sure. I was more worried about getting Ruthie out than looking to see what was on fire."

"Be careful. If they think the letters weren't destroyed, they could come looking for them."

Maxwell stared at her with a stony, determined gaze. "They almost hurt my Ruthie once. I won't let it happen again. Find out what her father was caught up in so we can get on with our lives."

"I will. Tell Ruthie, good night for me."

Shandra left the house, climbed into her Jeep, and headed home. But she wouldn't be sleeping for a bit. There was too much she wanted to find out on the internet before she could fall asleep.

~*~

Ryan pulled up to the address dispatch had given him for Chea Timms. It was a small single-story house built on the outskirts of Huckleberry. He'd checked and both she and her husband still taught school. Chea at Huckleberry Elementary and Mr. Timms at Warner High School. They didn't have children.

No dogs barked as he walked through a lawn with only a few scattered leaves on the short-cropped grass. Lights from the larger living room window spilled onto robust plants with multi-petaled flowers in autumn colors.

He didn't see a door bell. Two quick raps on the door

brought footsteps to the other side.

The knob turned and the door opened far enough to present a man of about sixty years of age. His graying hair was worn in two braids laying against a sky-blue pullover. He had on gray slacks and beaded moccasins.

"Mr. Timms?" Ryan asked.

"Yes. How may I help you?" Timms didn't offer to open the door any wider to allow him in.

"I'd like to speak with your wife, Chea." He pulled out his badge. "I'm Detective Ryan Greer with the Weippe County Sheriff's Department."

The man stepped back allowing entrance. "Why do you need to speak to my wife?"

Uncertain how much the man knew about his wife and the deceased, Ryan answered, "I have some more questions about the homicide that happened at Ruthie Kerby's wedding."

The man's eyes widened. "A homicide at Ruthie's wedding? Who was killed?"

"Your wife didn't tell you?" Now he wondered if the man knew his wife had been at the Huckleberry Police Station for questioning.

"No. She said Ruthie got cold feet and the wedding was canceled." Mr. Timms led him into the living room and motioned for him to take a seat. "My wife is in our room reading. I'll get her."

"Thank you." Ryan made a pretense to sit, but as soon as the man's back was to him, he started prowling the room, studying everything. Three teaching awards sat on the top shelf of a literature heavy book case. Many books were on the history of ancient weapons. One photo of the couple sat on a lower shelf. There were no photos of other family members. Not even, Nattie, Chea's mother.

The room was clean, immaculate, with a barely lived-in feel. He liked Shandra's open house plan with her paints and colored pencils, Sheba's toys, and now his personal items scattered around. It had a homey, lived-in feel. This house felt sterile.

He heard hushed voices and footsteps. Ryan strode to the chair he'd been invited to sit in and sat, pulling out his notepad.

Chea walked into the room. Fear had rounded her eyes and pinched her lips. Mr. Timms walked sternly beside her, motioning for her to take a seat on the couch closest to Ryan.

The woman sat, her hands folded primly in her lap.

Would the woman talk to him in front of her husband? From the panic in her eyes, he had a feeling her husband knew nothing about her fling with Donald Kerby before he came along.

"Mr. Timms, would you leave your wife and I alone. Although you stated you knew nothing of the homicide, I would rather question you separately to make sure you give me your version of what you know."

Relief swept over Chea's face, but Mr. Timms became angry.

"I am her husband. Whatever she has to say, I have a right to hear." Mr. Timms sat on the couch beside his wife.

"Let me state it this way then. I need answers from your wife and I don't believe she will answer them with you present."

Mr. Timms stared at Chea. She didn't return his gaze, continuing to stare at her folded hands.

"I see. Very well. I'll leave you two alone." Mr.

Timms stood.

"I do have one question for you. Why didn't you attend Ruthie's wedding?" Ryan watched the woman and not the man. She flinched.

"I had a meeting with the principal to go over the test scores of the incoming freshmen."

"On a Saturday?" He'd never heard of teachers working on weekends unless it was an extra-curricular activity.

"It was the only day we both had enough time to go over the testing thoroughly."

"Thank you." Ryan made a note to check with the principal about the meeting.

Once the man was out of the room, Ryan turned his full attention on Chea. "I want to know how you received the letters from Donald Kerby and what you did with them? Ruthie found the ones you left at the back door of the diner. There wasn't an address, which means you had to have received a letter, too."

"I told you before, Donald sent me the letters to give to Ruthie, but there wasn't a return address."

"Didn't you even look at the postmark? You know, the ink stamped up in the corner of the letter near the stamp?"

"I did, but they seemed to always come from different places. Like he had people who were traveling put them in a mailbox for him. One was from Michigan, one from San Francisco, another from Utah. I don't think they ever came from the same place." She put her hands palm up in her lap. "My husband doesn't know about Donald and I. He thinks I've only ever loved him."

Ryan shook his head. "I can't make any promises about your affair with the deceased not coming out. I have to follow all leads and ask everyone questions." He got back to the matter that brought him here. "What time did you put the box of letters behind Ruthie's Diner?"

Her gaze leveled on his. "I didn't take a box of letters to the diner."

"Where did you keep the letters?" If she hadn't taken the letters then who did?

"The letters have been hidden at my mother's house for over thirteen years. Once Ruthie turned eighteen they stopped coming. I'd hoped it meant Donald was returning." Chea twisted her fingers. "I waited as long as I could before I finally accepted Clarence's proposal. I was getting too old to hope for another man like Donald to come around."

"And Clarence never knew about Donald?" He found it hard to believe Chea and the victim kept their affair a secret in this small community.

"He knew there had been someone before him that I loved, but I've never told him who." She glanced up. "I don't think he'd mind, other than it had been a married man. Clarence believes in rules and order." She glanced around the room. "Anything that goes against those upsets him."

"Did your mother know about the letters?" He had to discover who'd put the letters on Ruthie's door step.

She shook her head. "I never told her about the letters or Donald and I. He didn't tell anyone because he was married and didn't know what his crazy wife would do if she found out."

"Someone found the letters and set them on the diner's kitchen steps for Ruthie to find. Twenty minutes later, someone tried to burn the diner down with her and Maxwell in it."

"Oh no!" Chea's hand covered her mouth. "Is she? Are they okay?"

"Maxwell got them out, but it means someone has been watching you or your mother and knew about the letters. That is the only explanation I can find for someone trying to torch the diner." He peered into her eyes. "Where were you at eight-twenty tonight?"

She blinked rapidly. "I was here. You don't think…"

"And your husband. Was he here as well?"

"He was. We were both here. We had dinner at six, went for a walk, and returned at seven-thirty. Then I went up to read while he worked on his class syllabus."

"Where did you keep the letters from Ruthie's father?"

She stopped a second as if debating whether to tell him. "In a shoe box, under a loose floorboard in my room."

Ryan stood. "Thank you for your time and answers. Tell your husband it was a pleasure meeting him." He walked to the door and let himself out.

It was after ten o'clock, but he had to follow the leads. He slipped into his pickup and dialed Shandra.

"Hello," she answered, before the phone had barely rang.

"You answered fast."

"The phone was sitting beside me. I've been going through the newspaper archives trying to figure out what could have been the thing that sent Donald on the run."

He smiled. Telling her to stay home didn't mean she'd stop trying to find the reason behind the murder and the fire. "What have you found?" He started the pickup and headed into town and down the main street toward Warner. Nattie Small lived north of town about five miles.

"The body found in Orin's car was that of Mark

Dapling, a known hitman. But there is nothing about who he might have been here to kill."

"I had Cathleen pull up the reports on the case. They're on my computer but I haven't had time to go through them." He steered onto the road leading to Nattie's. "Chea said she hadn't seen that box of letters in years. I'm headed to Nattie's now to see if she was the one who put the letters behind the diner."

"Let me know what happens."

"I will. Get some sleep."

"I've been thinking about that. If I'm lucky Ella will come to me in a dream and we'll have another clue." Shandra sighed. "See you when you get here."

"Hopefully, only another hour or so."

He hit the disconnect button and noticed a text. It was from Trapp. *Accelerant was gasoline thrown through the window in a glass jar with a rag on fire.* Ryan didn't like that it was something made at the spur of the moment and easy for anyone to have fashioned.

A dog barked as he pulled up to the small, batten board house. The flood light at the front door lit the yard up as a large scruffy dog ran across the porch. The lawn hadn't been mowed in a while. Wild plants and flowers grew haphazardly about the yard.

"Hey, boy. Are you friendly?" Ryan asked, stepping out of his vehicle.

"Dog, come!" Nattie's voice carried from behind the screen door.

"Mrs. Small, it's Detective Greer. I'd like a few words with you."

"Come on in. Dog won't bite ya. He's to scare ornery critters off. Ones that don't have enough sense to see if he's friendly.”

Ryan stepped through the screen door into a cluttered front room.

“Have a seat. I was just getting ready for my cup of chamomile tea. Would you care for some?” Nattie stood beside a door that led into what appeared to be the kitchen. She scratched at her right palm.

“I’m fine, thank you. Go ahead and get your tea.” He sat on an over-stuffed chair that looked to be as old as the woman. All of the furniture in the room was vintage and worn. Unlike her daughter’s house, the walls, shelves, and any place available had photographs. He spotted many of Ruthie as she’d grown up and just as many of Chea. There were a few of a younger Nattie with a handsome Native American man. The photo that caught his attention was one of the Timms’s wedding party. Neither the bride or the groom glowed with love for one another. They were both posed and looking as stoic as photos he’d seen of couples in the 1800s. It appeared their marriage was one of convenience and propriety and not of love.

“Here you go. You said you didn’t want tea, but I brought you some coffee.” Nattie handed the coffee mug to him and placed her cup and saucer on the table next to a small rocker. She sat down, smiled at him, and scratched her palms. “What brings you out here so late?”

“Did you find the letters from Donald Kerby to his daughter and take them to the diner tonight?” He knew the woman liked straight talk.

Her eyes narrowed. “There a law against leaving something for people to find?”

“No. But twenty minutes after the box was found, someone set the diner on fire.”

Her eyes widened and her gnarled hand raised to her mouth, much the same action as her daughter had done not thirty minutes before. "Oh my heavens! Is Ruthie alright?"

"She and Maxwell made it out. What I want to know is did you tell anyone you had found the box of letters and did you notice anyone watching you?" He studied the woman.

Her complexion had faded with his comment about the fire. Now it grew ruddier as her eyes glinted with anger. "That daughter of mine should not have kept the letters from Ruthie. All these years she thought her father had abandoned her. Zelda called me after you talked to her. She said you mentioned letters from Donald to Ruthie and wanted to know why I hadn't given them to Ruthie. I told her the truth. Because I didn't know they existed. That got me to thinking about letters Chea received after Donald left. They didn't have any return address. When I asked her about them, she said they were from students who had moved away." She waved a hand toward a door off the front room. "I went into Chea's old room and tore the place apart and found the shoe box under the boards in the closet. All the letters had Ruthie's name on them and they'd never been opened. I don't know if Donald sent Chea a letter, too, and she destroyed them, but I felt given her daddy was gone, Ruthie should have the letters."

"Why didn't you give them to her, instead of leaving them on the back step?" Ryan believed the woman.

Her face sagged and her eyes held sadness. "I didn't want Ruthie to think I'd kept the letters from her all those years. You don't know how that girl pined for her daddy to come home. She'd make wishes and pray for him to come back."

"Did you tell anyone about the letters?"

She shook her head. "I didn't tell anyone. I learned of the letters from you and then Zelda."

Which meant Ruthie's mother had to have mentioned them to someone. Considering her inebriated state when he'd questioned her, he was surprised she remembered he'd mentioned the letters.

"Thank you for your time, coffee, and information." Ryan stood.

"How bad was the diner damaged?" Nattie asked.

"I'm not sure of the damages." He walked to the door. "Giving those letters to Ruthie was the right thing to do. But someone thinks there is more in them than a father apologizing for leaving his little girl behind."

Chapter Twelve

Shandra rolled her shoulders and sat up straight. She'd been hunched over the computer for too long. Ryan should be arriving soon.

Sheba rose to her feet and walked down the hallway to the back door. Before Shandra could get the computer off her lap and her feet untangled from the blanket she'd wrapped around her legs, the big dog woofed to go outside.

"I'll be there in a minute." She stepped out of the blanket pooled around her feet and headed to the hallway. Sheba's wagging tail caused a breeze, sending chills across Shandra's exposed skin.

She opened the door and the dog bounded out into the cold evening air. A quick swing through the kitchen for a cup of hot cocoa and she returned to the couch. The notepad she'd used to scribble down her findings sat on the coffee table. She picked it up and leaned back. What was a hitman doing in Huckleberry in the '70s? The same time Donald Kerby worked for Mr. Narvel. They'd discovered during the murder of Mrs. Narvel that her husband had used mob money to build the ski resort and town. Perhaps a visit with Mr. and Mrs. Aducci was in order tomorrow.

Her eyes closed and she breathed in and out, ignoring the questions plaguing her mind. She drifted into that realm between consciousness and not quite sleep.

She stood on the edge of a cliff, staring into the unending gap below. Ella appeared, floating in the air above the abyss. "Grandmother, why am I here?" The wispy image pointed across the chasm to the other side. A man and woman argued. She couldn't tell who they were, only see the dark silhouettes against the blinding yellow of the sun. "Who are they Ella?" Someone snuck up behind the man. She saw the raised arm holding a revolver. "No! Don't!"

"Shandra, wake up. Shandra?" A hand shook her gently.

She slowly released the dream and came awake. Ryan's face came into view. A smile tugged her lips. "My dreams aren't so bad when I wake and see you."

He grinned. "Was this a dream with your grandmother?"

"Yes." She told him about the dream and how she'd felt the man was in danger. "I don't understand. Is it Maxwell who is in danger or was it showing me what happened that caused Donald Kerby to run?" She shook her head. "I'm so confused."

"Let's go to bed and tackle it in the morning." Ryan grasped her hand, helping Shandra to her feet.

"Did you find out who gave the letters to Ruthie?" She picked up her full cup of cocoa and headed for the kitchen.

"It was Nattie. Zelda called her asking about the

letters. Nattie didn't know about them but put things together and decided Chea did. She tore her daughter's room apart and found them."

"So was someone watching Nattie and knew the letters had been delivered?" Shandra spun from putting the cup in the sink. "Is Nattie now in danger?"

"I would guess someone learned about the letters from Zelda and her call to Nattie. Then someone watched Mrs. Small and followed her. Saw her put the box at the diner steps and couldn't get to it before you picked it up. To get rid of the letters, they improvised an easy accelerant and tossed it through the kitchen window. The only good thing is no one but Ruthie, Maxwell, you, and I, know the letters weren't burned."

Ryan maneuvered her back through the great room. Sheba raised her head from her bed by the fireplace. "Are you staying there?" Ryan asked.

The dog flopped her head back down.

"You must have let Sheba in when you came home." Shandra slipped into bed.

"I did." He went in the bathroom to take a shower and get ready for bed.

Shandra wanted to talk more about what they'd each learned but her eyes wouldn't stay open.

~*~

Shandra woke early the next morning. The dream she'd had while on the couch returned to her as she'd slept. This time she didn't shout. She waited to see what would happen. The man with the gun forced the man with the woman to leave. He didn't kill him.

She padded through the great room with Sheba trotting ahead of her. At the laundry room, Shandra asked, "Do you want fed or go outside?"

Sheba grabbed the handle on what was supposed to be a laundry bin but instead held the large bag of dog food.

"Breakfast it is." Shandra poured food into Sheba's bowl and refilled the two-quart water bowl.

In the kitchen, she started coffee brewing for Ryan and put the kettle on for her tea. By the time she had pancakes whipped up and the coffee had brewed, Ryan walked into the room.

"Smells good." He started to give her a morning hug when Sheba woofed. "I'll get that." He left the room to let the dog out.

Shandra set the stack of cooked pancakes on the counter along with butter and syrup. "Go ahead and start," she said when Ryan returned.

"Did you have any more dreams last night?" he asked, taking a seat on a stool.

"The same one as before, only I waited and the man with the weapon forced the other man to leave. Do you think it was Donald being forced to leave? But by who?" She sat down next to Ryan and placed a plate of fried eggs on the counter between them.

"It seems that he was forced to leave everyone he cared about behind when he left. If it had been something he wanted to do, I would have thought he'd have taken his wife and daughter or at least his lover and his daughter."

Shandra snapped her attention on Ryan. "Lover? Where did you learn that?"

Ryan mentally slapped himself. He hadn't meant for that to slip out. That's what came of talking over his cases with Shandra. He forgot this case needed to be kept to himself to avoid the wrong information getting out. Like that Donald had been fooling around with Ruthie's teacher. He shoved a big bite of pancake in his mouth.

Shandra peered at him with narrowed eyes. When he swallowed, she launched. "Who was Donald Kerby's lover? How did you find out? Why didn't you tell me before?"

He held up a hand, palm toward her. "Whoa. I'm the officer working the case. I don't have to tell you everything I learn."

The warm amber eyes he'd found so interesting when they'd met were now giving off an icy glow. "Since when have you started not telling me everything? We work together as a team even though your superiors don't know that. Or have you decided that my dreams and the information you gather can't be meshed together to find the truth anymore?"

Ryan dropped his fork and grasped her right hand. "I believe in your dreams and your ability to ferret out the truth, but in this case, you are close to Ruthie. I didn't want you having to lie to her or Maxwell because I gave you information that would upset her."

She stared into his eyes. "That's why you didn't tell me about the lover? To make sure Ruthie didn't find out?"

"Yes. You know I don't lie or withhold anything from you. But in this case, I'm not only protecting you, I'm protecting Ruthie." He ducked his head then peered into her eyes. "I care about you and I care about Ruthie. You two are good friends. I don't want this investigation to come between you."

She leaned forward and kissed his lips. "Okay, I'll let this little secret you have stay that way. For Ruthie's sake."

"Thank you."

Shandra picked up her fork, moving pieces of pancake around on her plate. "But if you found out about the lover, won't Ruthie?"

"According to my source, the affair was kept very quiet, because of Ruthie. I've been guaranteed no one knew about it." He put another bite in his mouth.

"Someone knows. What about Zelda? Wouldn't she know if her husband was fooling around?" She gave him a sideways glance. "I'd know if you were."

He swallowed the bite with a chaser of coffee. "You would know because you are an observant woman who can tell when people aren't being natural. However, with Zelda, you're talking about a woman who was drunk or high most of the time. I doubt she even knew when her husband was home or when he was gone."

"True. But this is a small community. Someone would have noticed Donald's car always at someone's house or a motel."

"I've had the same thoughts. It's something I need to ask the person in question." He slipped off the stool. "Gotta go. I need to talk with Zelda this morning. If she is the only one besides Chea and Nattie to know about the letters, she had to have slipped about them to someone. I need to find out her hang outs and see who frequents them. You up for a date night when I find out what bars she haunts?"

"I'll take a date night with you any time, even if we're looking for perps."

Ryan laughed at Shandra's attempt to sound like a policeman. "I'll come pick you up about six."

"I'll be ready."

"What are you doing today?" Ryan asked.

She was in between projects which meant she was

waiting for an idea to hit for her next vase. Some days she rode the mountain, some days she sat in the sun with a sketch pad.

"I'm going to check on Ruthie and Maxwell and help them clean up the diner if that's all that needs done."

"Be careful. We don't know if there will be any more attempts on them. I'll have the sheriff put out a press release that a box of letters from Ruthie's deceased father burned in the blaze. That will keep them safe."

Shandra threw her arms around him. "Thank you! I've been worrying about those two ever since I saw Maxwell carry Ruthie out of the smoking diner."

"You're welcome. See you tonight." He kissed her lips and headed to the great room. He picked up his computer bag, grabbed his coat, and headed out to his work vehicle. After talking with Zelda, he would track down Orin Kerby. He had a sneaking suspicion the man was behind everything that had happened to his brother.

Chapter Thirteen

Ryan talked to Sheriff Oldham while driving to Cotton. The man had agreed to release a story about the letters being burned in the fire. They didn't want more bodies on their hands.

It was ten when Ryan parked his car in front of Mrs. Kerby's house. The house was small, square, and run down. The windows didn't look as if they'd ever been cleaned. He stepped out of his SUV and walked up to the door. The yard was dry grass and weeds up to his knees.

He heard rustling noises and footsteps retreating behind the door. Scanning the drive and the street in front, he didn't see any other cars. From the sound he would say, Zelda had company.

Three more strong raps on the door and she called out, "I'm comin'."

His attention was riveted to the sounds in the house. The shuffling of slippers on linoleum grew louder. The knob turned, and Zelda, looking as if she'd drank all the alcohol in a liquor store peered at him with blood-shot eyes.

"What do you want?" she asked, without a glimmer of recognition.

"I'm Detective Greer, we spoke yesterday about your husband's death. I have some more questions."

The sound of someone trying to move a stubborn window or door echoed down the hallway. He promptly moved her to the side and entered the house, hurrying down the hallway, his hand on the handle of his revolver.

He found an African American male in his sixties, trying to fit through a window large enough for a man half his size.

The man glanced toward Ryan. The face was older, but it was Orin Kerby.

"Stop! Get back in here." Ryan grabbed the man by the back of his shirt and dragged him back into the room. "Why were you running?"

The man glared at him and clamped his lips together.

"Come on. You can listen to this conversation, then I have questions for you." Ryan pushed the man ahead of him into the living room. Zelda appeared to be asleep on the couch. "Sit," he ordered Orin and pointed to a chair.

Once the man was seated, Ryan walked over and shook the woman by her shoulder. "Mrs. Kerby. Zelda, wake up. I need to ask you some important questions." He shook her some more and her eyelids lurched open as if her eyeballs had dry spots that caught on her lids.

"Zelda, this is important. Someone tried to kill Ruthie last night."

"What?" Orin came up out of the chair. "Who did? Why?" He moved to the couch and pulled Zelda up off the cushions. "Wake up woman. Your girl is in trouble." Orin shook her harder than Ryan had.

"Go away, I got a headache." Zelda swat at Orin's hand.

"How long have you been staying with Zelda?" Ryan asked. The man was sober. Maybe he could answer the questions.

Orin's gaze held distrust.

"I'm only trying to find the answers to who killed your brother and attempted to kill your niece."

"I've been here off and on since I got out of prison. Been tryin' to find a job." He shook his head. "No one wants to hire an ex-con."

"I'm sorry to hear that. What I need to know is, why did your brother leave? And why didn't he take his wife and daughter?"

The man eyed him. "What's this got to do with his death and Ruthie?"

"I don't know. Maybe nothing, but I can't find a reason why anything in the present could have been a reason to kill him. But there are a lot of things in his past, before he left here, that doesn't make sense and could have been the catalyst for his death." Ryan flipped open his notepad. "You went to jail for having a dead hitman in the trunk of your car. Did you kill him or did your brother?"

"Neither one of us killed the man. We was cleaning up for someone else when I was pulled over." He shook his head. "I knew taking the rap for the killing would be better for me than telling who really did it." Orin glanced over at Zelda. "I figured it was better for Zelda and Ruthie if Donald disappeared. That way the person we was working for wouldn't think they knew anything. That night when the police gave me one call, I called Donald and told him to run and don't look back if he wanted to live and wanted his family to live."

"Were you covering for Mr. Narvel?" Ryan had looked at his notes from the trial and where the brothers had worked. Orin had been a driver for Mr. Narvel, and Donald had been a handyman at the resort and helped around the Narvel house.

Orin nodded. "He's dead now and can't do us no harm. But there's others that are still alive."

"Like Vince Barsotti?"

The man's jaw dropped. "That old man is still kicking?"

"He isn't, but Vince Barsotti Junior is."

"Did you know about the letters your brother sent to Ruthie?" Ryan had to discover how Barsotti had found out about them. He had to have been the person responsible for the fire. It was the only thing that made sense.

"Not until Zelda was talking to someone on the phone about them. She was upset that Donald sent letters to Ruthie and only sent her money without anything saying where he was or when he'd be back." Orin shook his head and stared at the woman emitting an unbecoming snore. "I told Donald before he married Zelda, she was going to be a handful. But they'd fooled around and she became pregnant. He wasn't going to let her raise his child alone." He laughed. "That was the one thing he kept saying when I told him he had to leave. I can't leave Ruthie alone with Zelda." He waved a hand toward a photo on a table. Nattie Small, Chea, and Ruthie had their arms around each other's shoulders and smiled into the camera. "Those two turned out to be the best thing that ever happened to that poor kid."

Ryan had to believe Donald's affair hadn't been just for him. He'd found a woman who would help him look out for his daughter.

"Back to the letters. Have you seen anyone hanging around here? Maybe watching the place?" He waited a beat. When Orin looked as if he were thinking, Ryan added, "Maybe in a dark sedan?"

"I did see a couple of younger men sitting down the block in a dark blue sedan a couple of days ago."

"Before or after the wedding?" Ryan finally had a solid lead.

"Both. But not the day of the wedding. I was out walking and didn't see the car."

"Why didn't you go to the wedding?" Ryan had to discover more about the car and its occupants.

"I wasn't invited, and Zelda told me that Ruthie didn't know she had an uncle. Her wedding didn't seem like the place to introduce myself."

Ryan had an idea. "If you're looking for work, you might want to introduce yourself to Ruthie and offer to help her clean up the diner. I'm not sure how much damage the fire caused, but she could use the help."

Orin grinned. "I'd like that."

"Can you think of anything else you remember about the car or the people inside?" He could put out an all points on the car if he had something more than dark blue sedan.

"It had out of state plates. Washington, I think. That's why I didn't think too much of it. Figured they were here visiting relatives, maybe waiting for them to get home."

"Thank you. I also need to know where Zelda likes to go to drink. I need to find out if she's been telling people in the bars about the letters. I have to find out how someone knew about them." Ryan was also looking forward to taking Shandra on a sort of date. They hadn't been out just the two of them in a while. All the wedding craziness of her friends had them attending functions rather than quiet nights alone.

~*~

Shandra called Mrs. Aducci as soon as she was dressed. It was Monday and the married couple spent the one day Rigatoni's was closed driving to pick up supplies. She wanted to catch them before they left.

"Shandra, what a pleasant surprise," Mrs. Aducci said.

"I'm glad you feel that way. I was wondering, if I hurried down to Huckleberry, would you and your husband meet me at the donut shop before you head to get supplies? I have some questions for you." Shandra had her fingers crossed the woman would be willing to talk with her.

"Of course. We always have time for Miranda's friends. We'll see you in an hour at Daily Donut."

Shandra hung up from that call and walked out to the barn to get her Jeep.

"Where are you goin'?" Lil asked, walking out of the tack room with Lewis around her neck.

"I'm checking on Ruthie and Maxwell, then meeting Mrs. Aducci at the Daily Donut. Would you like to come along?" She opened the Jeep door.

"No. I have things to do. But you could bring me back a few of those donuts with the jelly in the middle." The woman smacked her lips.

"I can do that. See you later. Sheba is out in the woods somewhere." Shandra started up the Jeep and headed down her drive.

Once the tires were crunching on the gravel county road, she dialed Ruthie.

"Hello Shandra," her friend answered.

"Hi. How are you and Maxwell this morning?" Shandra dodged a pothole in the road.

"Glad to be alive. We're getting ready to head in to assess the damage to the diner. We'll know what our options are after we see how much was destroyed. I've already been on the phone with an insurance appraiser. He's meeting us there."

"Good. I'm headed to the Daily Donut to visit with Mr. and Mrs. Aducci. I'll drop by the diner and take you and Maxwell to lunch at the lodge."

"You don't have to do that," Ruthie said.

"I want to. I feel bad you missed your honeymoon and now you don't have a diner. Let me treat you. I'll see you later." She hung up before Ruthie came up with an excuse to get out of lunch.

She passed her friend's driveway and continued on down the county road. The next driveway down from Ruthie and Maxwell's a dark blue sedan was parked with the nose headed out. The driveway went to a house owned by people who were only there during the summer months. She'd asked the couple before they'd left if they planned to rent it out this winter and they'd said no. The renters the year before had done too much damage.

She hit the number one on her phone. It went to Ryan's voice mail. She stopped down the road around a corner where the occupants of the car couldn't see her and scrolled through her contacts for Maxwell's number.

"Hey, what are you doing calling me?" he answered, the question in his voice was clear. Why him and not

Ruthie.

"There is a car that looks like the one I saw drive into the alley last night, sitting in the Laron's driveway. I wanted to warn you. I tried to call Ryan but it went to voicemail. I'm going to call nine-one-one and report a suspicious vehicle. Can you keep Ruthie there a while longer? At least until the police have chased them away?"

"I will. Don't you go talking to them."

"I won't."

She hung up and dialed 9-1-1.

"What's your emergency?" asked the dispatcher.

"I'm Shandra Higheagle. My friends were nearly killed last night in a fire. I saw what we think was the car driven by the person who threw gas into their diner. Right now, the same car is sitting in the driveway before theirs. It's a summer residence and no one should be there. It's ten miles up County Road Fifteen."

"I'll send a deputy out right away. Please stay on the line."

She was going to be late meeting the Aduccis, but Ruthie and Maxwell's lives mattered more.

Chapter Fourteen

Ryan climbed into his vehicle in time to hear dispatch report a suspicious vehicle ten miles out County Road 15. That was right before Maxwell and Ruthie's new place. He called into dispatch. "What is the description of the car?" He put his car into gear, flicked on his lights and sirens and headed as fast as he could back to Huckleberry.

"The person who called in says it is a dark blue sedan with a Washington plate. We're running the plates now. Deputy Speaks is only five minutes away."

"I'm headed there, too. I just learned that car is part of my homicide investigation." He hung up and roared down Huckleberry Street and out the other side of town onto County Road 15.

He shut down the siren and turned off the lights five miles out. At nine miles, he slowed down and spotted Shandra's Jeep sitting to the side of the road. She must have called the car in.

Ryan stopped his vehicle next to hers and rolled the

windows down. "Did you call the suspicious car in?"

"Yes. It's the one I saw go down the alley behind the diner last night." She nodded on up the road. "Ron Speaks is up there now."

"I'll go back him up. You stay put."

She nodded.

He continued up the road. Speaks had two men standing spread eagle against the side of a dark blue sedan. Ryan stopped behind the county car and walked up to help him out.

"What did you find?" Ryan asked, taking out his cuffs and cuffing the short man with scraggly long hair and a beard.

"These two refused to give their names or state their business," Speaks said, pulling the larger of the two men away from the vehicle.

"That's fine. We'll print them before I question them. Take them to Huckleberry PD. I'll be right along."

They tucked both men into the back of the county car. Speaks drove off and Ryan snapped photos of the car, opening the doors and the trunk. He found food wrappers, empty drink cans, and glass jars and rags in the back of the trunk. There wasn't a fuel can but the trunk reeked of gasoline and there was a stain on the carpet.

Shandra drove up as he was snapping photos of the trunk. She stepped out of the Jeep and walked over. "Did they tell you anything?"

"No. I didn't expect them to. They have carried gasoline around in the back of this car." His phone vibrated on his hip. Dispatch.

"Greer."

"It's Cathleen. We've identified the owner of the

sedan."

"I have too. The registration is to a Toby Brown."

"He's wanted for several arsons and a couple of murders in the Seattle area. It's noted he does odd jobs for Vince Barsotti."

Ryan had figured as much. "Thanks. I'm taking photos of the car. Send a tow truck to pick it up and have someone cut the stain out of the carpet in the trunk and send it to the lab. I'm pretty sure they've carried gasoline."

"I'll get that done. Do you plan to come over Halloween and help hand out candy?"

This was the only problem with having a sister who worked the county dispatch. She knew his schedule and life. "I doubt it. This case will keep me busy."

"You know your nephews like to try and scare you."

"Not this year. Maybe next." He hung up and turned his attention to Shandra who was peering into the back seat of the vehicle.

"What are you doing? Don't touch anything. This will be checked for prints. Someone gave the victim a ride to the wedding." Ryan pulled Shandra away from the car and shut the door.

"They had a lot of food wrappers and containers in there. It's like they've been living in the car." She pulled out her phone.

"Who are you calling and where were you going?" Ryan asked, closing all the doors on the vehicle.

"I was headed to meet Mr. and Mrs. Aducci at the Daily Donut." She held up a finger. "Hi Mark, this is Shandra Higheagle." She smiled and nodded. "Please tell them I'm running behind and should be there in ten minutes. Thanks." She pushed a button, scrolled, and poked the screen. "Hi Maxwell. The people in the car are headed to the police station. You can leave now." She smiled. "Tell her it was for her own good. See you at lunch."

Shandra shoved the phone into her pocket and faced him. "When I saw the car, I called Maxwell and told him to keep Ruthie at home, that I was calling nine-one-one."

Ryan put his arm around her. "I'm glad you spotted the car and had the presence to call both Maxwell and the police. But I'm even happier that you stayed away and let the authorities handle things." All his lecturing on letting the police handle things may have finally paid off.

Shandra smiled at Ryan. She had done some impulsive things in the past, mostly when she believed he was in danger. But today, it had been easy to stay out of the way and let the police deal with things. If the car had moved, she would have followed. She'd been on the phone with the dispatch the whole time waiting for the police.

"I need to go. Have fun questioning those two." She strode to her Jeep and stepped up into the vehicle.

Ryan followed her. "Why are you meeting the Aduccis?"

"I read more newspaper articles on Orin Kerby's trial and conviction and had some question for them, since they would have been here during that time." She started the engine.

"If you learn anything, call me." He closed the door and she gave him nod.

Now that the threat to Ruthie and Maxwell was out of the way and the people who possibly killed Mr. Kerby were at the police station, she felt as if a weight had been lifted. Miranda had invited her and Ryan to a Halloween party tomorrow night. She had a feeling they'd now be able to attend. That meant, she would need to find costumes this afternoon, since she'd put it off due to the wedding preparations.

She sped down the county road and slipped into the first parking spot she could find close to the bakery. The Daily Donut was a favorite of the locals and the out-of-towners.

Mr. and Mrs. Aducci were sitting at a small round table by the window. She waved to them and walked through the door.

"I'm sorry I'm late." She took a seat.

Mrs. Aducci slid a cup of hot cocoa across the table towards her. "I knew you liked cocoa but did not know which donut you liked."

"Thank you!" Shandra held the cup in her hands and sipped.

The older couple smiled and watched her. They had been like family to her ever since she moved to the Huckleberry area. The Aducci's and their daughter Miranda had taken her in the first time she walked into their restaurant, Rigatoni's.

"You must be curious about why I wanted to talk to you," she started.

"We were wondering. The last time we met this way you asked about the Narvels." Mr. Aducci, picked up his coffee cup. "Is that what you wish to talk about again?"

She nodded. "I know Mrs. Narvel was your friend." Shandra directed this comment to Mrs. Aducci. "It's Mr. Narvel and some people who worked for him that I have questions about this time."

"We didn't really spend much time with either of the Narvels," Mr. Aducci said.

"But you lived here at the time and you heard things. The man, Ruthie Kerby's father, who was killed this past weekend at my ranch, he worked for Mr. Narvel before he left. His brother, Orin, was Mr. Narvel's driver. He was arrested for killing a hitman. That same night, Ruthie's dad left, never to be seen again until Ruthie's wedding, Saturday. There has to be a connection." Shandra picked up the cocoa and took another sip as the couple glanced at one another.

Mrs. Aducci cleared her throat. "The Kerby brothers were nice men. They grew up in the area and helped us with some of the building of our restaurant."

"Donald, Ruthie's father, he helped me with the living quarters above the restaurant. He was a good builder," Mr. Aducci said. "I told him about Mr. Narvel needing help at the big Victorian. Mrs. Kerby back then spent a lot on drinking."

"And drugs, I heard." Mrs. Aducci pinched her lips and nodded her head.

Shandra had an idea. "Did you ever see Donald with another woman?"

Mrs. Aducci tapped her index finger against her lips. "Yes. A couple of times, months before he left, he and Chea Small, now Timms, were in the restaurant for dinner. They always talked about Ruthie. How she was doing in school."

An idea sprung from this. Could Chea have been Donald's lover Ryan slipped about? He'd been speaking with her a lot and her mother had the letters for Ruthie. "So they talked about Ruthie. It was like a father conferencing with his daughter's teacher?"

Mrs. Aducci nodded, then shook her head. "They

touched a lot under the table.”

“How would you know that?” Mr. Aducci asked.

“I was the hostess and waitressed back then. You can see more than you want sometimes. They touched legs and would eat with only one hand on the table. They may have been doing more than talking about Ruthie.” The older woman glanced at her husband. “It is how I figured out there was more between our Miranda and Alex.”

Mr. Aducci snorted. “They may be married but that doesn’t mean I have to like the idea.”

His wife patted his arm. “My Silvio thinks our new son-in-law thinks too highly of himself. I tell him, the man has been taught to think that way, but he loves our daughter. That is what matters.”

“He does love your daughter. Will you be at the Halloween party tomorrow night?” Shandra asked.

“Yes,” said Mrs. Aducci.

“No,” said Mr. Aducci. “We have a restaurant to run.”

His wife waved her hand. “That is what employees are for.”

Shandra smiled and pulled the conversation back to what she wanted to know. “Do you think Orin killed the man he was accused of killing?”

Mr. Aducci shook his head. “None of the Kerbys would kill anything. I never figured out why Orin went to jail.”

“Why would a hitman be here in Huckleberry back then?” She decided to focus on the man who’d been killed.

“The only person who someone might want dead back then would have been Mr. Narvel. He ran the town and had us all working for him.” Mr. Aducci drank the last of his coffee and put the cup down. “We need to go. There is much shopping to do for a restaurant."

"I'm sorry I kept you this long. Thank you for meeting me." Shandra stood.

Mrs. Aducci hugged her and whispered in her ear, "See you tomorrow night."

Shandra hugged her back.

When the couple left the bakery, Shandra walked over to the counter and bought six jelly donuts and six chocolate frosted with sprinkles. She put the donuts in the Jeep, locked it, and walked the two blocks down Huckleberry Street to Ruthie's Diner.

On her way by Dimensions Gallery, she peeked in the window to see if her friend Naomi might be roaming about the gallery floor. She wasn't, but her husband Ted was. He waved Shandra to come into the gallery.

She opened the big glass door and stood a moment, taking in the visual of the paintings, sculptures, and pottery that filled the gallery. Ted and Naomi Norton had been the first gallery she'd placed her work in when she moved to Huckleberry. They had become good friends and continued to showcase her work.

"Did you hear what happened to Ruthie's last night?" Ted asked, hurrying to her side.

"I was there and saw it." Shandra shuddered, thinking of how close she and her friends came to being caught in the fire.

"Naomi is over there now, seeing if she can help." Ted led her to an area where the morning light streamed through the large plate glass windows. Her latest vase sat on a four-foot-tall pedestal with the light glinting off the metallic embellishments she'd added to the rim and slashed across the sides. "What do you think?" Ted asked.

"You always find the best way to show off my work." She was pleased that the couple loved her work so much.

"We only enhance what you've already done."

"Thank you. I really need to get going. I'll talk to Naomi at Ruthie's." She strode out of the gallery.

Crossing the street, her heart lunged into her throat. The outside of the building that housed the diner had streaks of black coming out of the upstairs broken windows. The windows on the first floor were blackened on the inside.

People bustled in and out of the building hauling things. Many of the people she recognized as locals. All the charred furniture stood in a pile in front of the diner. Two men were throwing it in the back of a garbage truck.

She sidestepped a man carrying out charred wood.

Inside, she found Maxwell using a crowbar to pry the charred wood from the walls. Shandra spotted Ruthie through a hole in the wall between the seating area and the kitchen. She, Naomi, and Miranda were washing the pots and pans in the sink that was the only shiny thing in the kitchen.

"I'm here to help," she said, making the three women spin her direction.

"What took you so long," Miranda quipped.

"Oh things." Shandra made eye contact with Ruthie. "Where do you want me to start?"

"I wish we could go upstairs and check out the living quarters, but the fire marshal and our insurance agent told us not to go up. They said the timbers and flooring could have been compromised." Ruthie sighed. "I hope the firefighters didn't ruin my photo albums."

Shandra picked up a bucket. "How about you fill this

with soap and water and I'll start wiping down the appliances?"

Chapter Fifteen

Ryan entered the Huckleberry Police Station and was handed a sheet of papers.

"What's this?" he asked Officer Blane.

"The information on the two men Deputy Speaks brought in." He was grinning like he'd collared a serial killer.

"That was fast."

"When we put in the name of the owner on the vehicle registration, it popped up Toby Brown. The photo matched. The information in the system said he had priors with Doobie Smith. Put his name in, and boom, there was the other guy. Pulled up their priors."

"Who is in the interview room?" Ryan glanced through the list of priors.

"Doobie. He seemed like the slowest of the two." Blane winked and walked back to his desk.

Ryan shook his head. The young man had a lot to learn about police work, but he'd pulled together the paperwork

Ryan needed for his questioning.

He entered the interview room. Doobie was sitting in the chair, his arms to his sides, his gaze on a spot on the ceiling. Speaks stood inside the door watching him.

"I want a lawyer," Doobie said when Ryan sat in the chair across from him.

"Deputy Speaks would you bring a phone in here so Mr. Smith can make a phone call?" Ryan watched the scrawny, dirty man in front of him.

"How did you know my name?"

"Toby told me. He said you were the one with the idea to torch the diner last night." Ryan had to get the man talking before Speaks came back with a phone. He knew the deputy would take his time, but he didn't know how gullible Smith was going to be.

"That was his idea. I wanted to go in and take that box from them."

"What box?" Ryan asked.

His small dilated eyes bounced around in his eyes sockets. "The box. The one the old broad talked about."

"What was in the box? Money? Jewelry?" Ryan's mind went to the man's unkept hair and the thought when he shook, fleas could fly out.

Smith shook his head, but not vigorously. "Naw. Something the boss wanted destroyed."

"Boss? Toby said he was the boss." Ryan didn't mind using misinformation to make a killer or thief talk.

The man laughed, showing nasty brown teeth. He not only didn't take baths, it appeared he didn't take care of his teeth either. But then, he'd been living in a car.

"Toby ain't no boss. He bosses me around, but he don't call the shots. Mr. Barsotti does." As if saying the name jogged his memory, the man's face paled and his eyes searched the room. "You ain't going to tell anyone I said that, are you?"

"It's just between you and me. Why did the boss want the box?" Ryan could be this man's friend until he got the information he needed.

"Don't know. He just said, get the box and destroy it." He grinned. "We didn't get it, but we destroyed it."

"You set a business on fire. That's arson."

"We didn't kill no one. We seen them leave the building. All three of 'em."

A shiver raced up Ryan's spine. Shandra had just stepped out of the building they'd set on fire. He was surprised they hadn't noticed her Jeep drive by them this morning.

"Why were you still watching Ruthie Kerby this morning if you destroyed the box?"

The man clamped his mouth shut.

What made watching Ruthie more of a threat to him than torching the restaurant? This man had given him good evidence, but he had a feeling he wasn't the one who they'd get to turn on Barsotti. He didn't know the reason behind any of the things he did. They needed evidence to prove Barsotti was behind the hitman after Narvel and the one who killed Kerby.

"Did you and Toby go to the wedding on Saturday and kill a man?" Ryan studied Doobie closely.

"We didn't kill no one. We was following the old broad. We were told her daughter was getting married and to see if the father showed up." Doobie sat up. "We didn't know it was him when we first seen him. He was in a car with a younger woman when they came to the wedding.

She stopped a short ways up the driveway to the wedding. Then she took off again. Later we heard the father of the bride was killed. We didn't do it."

Ryan now knew how Donald had arrived at the wedding. Which meant he had to have contacted Chea to know about the wedding and to take him there. Why had she left that out?

Speaks entered at that moment with a phone. He plugged it into a jack in the wall.

"Take the phone away and escort Mr. Doobie to a cell. He's under arrest for arson."

"Hey, you said— "

"I said I wouldn't mention what you said to Mr. Barsotti, I didn't say I wouldn't arrest you." Ryan waved for Speaks to take the man away. He checked the recording device that had been sitting on the table. It had recorded the whole session.

Blane popped his head in the door. "Ready for the next one?"

"Yes." Scanning Toby Brown's priors, Ryan knew this man wouldn't be as easy to trick into spilling information.

The door opened and Blane escorted the taller, broader shouldered man into the room. He had a short, military haircut. His clothes were also reminiscent of military clothes. Drab green pants, black T-shirt, even military boots. This was the brains and the brawn of the two.

"Mr. Brown, have a seat." Ryan motioned to the seat across the table from him.

"I want a lawyer." The man's tone was as clipped and demanding as any drill sergeant Ryan had in the military.

"Officer Blane, would you please bring a phone in for Mr. Brown to call his lawyer?"

Blane grinned and stepped out of the room.

"Mr. Brown, I'll be recording this conversation." Ryan clicked the button on the recording machine.

The man crossed his arms and glared.

"Your partner, Doobie, said it was your idea to torch the diner last night." Ryan saw the man's jaw twitch.

"He also said you were both working for a Mr. Vince Barsotti."

A fist hit the table. "That little snitch! I knew I shouldn't have brought him along."

"What exactly did Mr. Barsotti tell you to do?"

Silence. The man had crossed his arms again.

"Why did you kill Donald Kerby?"

"I didn't kill anyone." The man remained with crossed arms and his dark eyes glared.

"But you were sent here to see if Donald Kerby showed up to his daughter's wedding. And he ended up dead. I don't find that a coincidence." Ryan spread the list of Toby's priors across the table. "You have a long list of arson, assaults, and your wanted for questioning in connection with a homicide or two in Seattle. I could put in a good word for you if you come clean about killed Kerby."

"I didn't kill no one."

"You didn't see him, walk up behind him, and slug him in the side of the head with a branch or a wooden post?" Ryan didn't like giving away the weapon but he had to see this man's reaction.

"I only saw the man when he arrived with the woman."

"Then how do you know he was the man you were looking for?" Ryan had caught him.

Brown swore under his breath. "I followed him through the trees. He went in the house. Then came out again, avoiding the people waiting in the barn."

"You followed him behind the barn and killed him."

"No. The bride came running out of the house. I ducked back around the side and waited. When I was going to follow, another woman came running toward the house, then a big black man, another woman…" he narrowed his eyes. "And you. There were too many people wandering around, looking for the bride. I left."

"Did you see anything when you left?" As much as he didn't want to believe the man, he did.

"Nothing. But before we got back to town a car sped by us."

"What kind?"

"Your average four door sedan."

"The color?"

"Cream or gold. Couldn't tell it was covered in dust."

Blane entered with the phone.

"Put Mr. Brown in a cell and book him on arson." Ryan stood and walked out of the room. While Vince Barsotti was trying to cover his tracks from a hit gone wrong twenty some years ago, he didn't think the man or his goons had anything to do with Donald Kerby's murder. Which meant it was someone local.

Chapter Sixteen

It was one o'clock when Shandra rounded up Maxwell, Ruthie, and Miranda to go to lunch. Everyone was dirty and smelled of smoke. They didn't want to go to the Huckleberry Lodge. Monday was the day Rigatoni's was closed and with Ruthie's out of commission there was only the Lodge or Maxie's bar.

They all washed up the best they could and sloshed the block and a half in wet shoes to Maxie's for a burger.

Maxine greeted them as they walked through the door. Her strawberry blonde hair was piled high and her double D breasts stretched the front of her skin-tight teal t-shirt. Teal, blue, and orange paisley print leggings clung to her shapely legs. "Have you all been camping?" she asked, getting a whiff of the smoke that clung to them from digging around in the soggy, burnt building.

"Ruthie! Give me a hug. My God, doll, first your father and now your diner." The woman wrapped her arms around Ruthie, hugging her tight. "If you need anything you let me know," she said, releasing her hold.

One thing about Maxine, she said what she thought and had a heart as large as her bra cup.

"Thanks, Maxine." Ruthie waved to the biggest table in the corner of the place. "We're starving from cleaning up the diner. You have any burger specials?"

Shandra followed her friends to the corner table and sat.

"We have the bacon cheeseburger as the special today," Maxine said, bringing over a tray of glasses filled with water.

Everyone said that would work for them, and Maxine hurried back to the kitchen.

"You're still coming to the Halloween party tomorrow night, aren't you?" Miranda asked.

It would be the first big party she'd held at her new husband's family home, the old Victorian house on the way to the ski resort. It was the perfect house for a Halloween party. Not only was it old and a bit on the spooky side at night, there had been a murder there less than six months earlier—Dr. Porter's aunt.

"If Ryan isn't working, we'll be there." Shandra glanced over at Maxwell and Ruthie. "You two should come. It will take your minds off all your troubles this week."

Maxwell picked up Ruthie's hand. "We could use some fun this week. What to do you say, Ruthie?"

"Come on. You don't want to miss the party. We'll have grown up games, food, and drinks. And I have a special prize for the best costume." Miranda sang the last sentence.

"I could use some fun," Ruthie said.

"Good! I want all my friends there." Miranda smiled. "Alex has planned something special for entertainment."

"Nothing scary or gory I hope," Shandra said, her mind instantly grasping onto the image of Ruthie's father slumped against her corral post.

"No. He said it would be fun for everyone to see." She picked at a napkin. "But he wouldn't even tell me what it was."

"That sounds ominous." Maxwell picked up his water. "If you want spooky, I can bring a coffin."

Shandra spit out the drink she'd taken. "I don't think so."

He grinned. "It was always a hit for parties when I was a kid."

"You're used to being around coffins and dead people since your father, and now you, are morticians." Shandra used her napkin to wipe up the water she'd spit.

Maxine returned with their burgers and a large basket of fries. "We're having a Halloween bash here tomorrow night. You're all invited."

"Thank you for the invite," Miranda said. "We'll be at my house, partying." She smiled. "I'll never get used to that. My house." She cringed. "You know what I mean, mine and Alex's house."

Maxine laughed. "You newlyweds are always so cute. But wait. That newness wears off and all you're left with is a man you wonder how the heck you liked enough to marry." She walked away and they all stared after her.

"Wow. She was a downer," Miranda said, plucking a fry out of the basket.

"Her husband blew into town, swept her off her feet, and turned out to be worthless. He didn't want to work, gambled, and Maxine almost lost this place to pay his debts." Ruthie glanced over at the woman wiping down the bar. "I can understand her animosity." She glanced at Maxwell. "Good thing I have a man who isn't afraid of work, has his own business, and would die rather than hurt me."

"You got that right." Maxwell kissed Ruthie, while Shandra and Miranda stared at their burgers.

Shandra cleared her throat and the two separated. "What did the insurance have to say about the building?"

"We should be able to get enough from them to get the place cleaned up and rebuilt. It's the structural issues I'm worried about. If we can't go up the stairs to assess the damage, how do we get compensated for it?" Ruthie picked up her burger.

"I've been thinking about that," Maxwell said. "I know someone who has one of those drones with a camera. I'll see if he'll loan it to me tomorrow."

Shandra's phone played a jazz tune. She glanced at the screen. Ryan. She stood and walked out the door of the bar.

"Hello."

"Hey good-looking. I'm calling to cancel our night out. We don't need to go bar hopping." The regret in Ryan's voice made her smile.

"You must have learned something from the two men."

"I did. They heard Mrs. Kerby ranting in the bar about the box of letters. They were sent here to contact Kerby, but I believe their story. They didn't kill him."

She sucked in air. "If they didn't then who did?"

"Still working on that. They did start the fire at the diner. They've been arrested for arson." He sighed. "Where are you?"

"With Ruthie, Maxwell, and Miranda at Maxie's having a burger. You want to join us?"

"I better not. I don't have answers for Ruthie and I don't want to disappoint her."

She understood. They all loved Ruthie and wanted to give her closure. "I understand. I told Miranda we'd be at her Halloween party tomorrow night. What kind of a costume do you want?"

He huffed. "I have always hated Halloween. No one is who you think they are. Just make sure it isn't some cartoon character."

She didn't know this about Ryan. She'd always liked Halloween because she could dress up as anyone or thing she wanted. "I'll do my best to come up with a dignified costume for you."

He laughed. "See you at home."

The line went dead and she returned to her friends.

"Who was that?" Miranda asked.

"Ryan. We were supposed to go out tonight but he had to cancel."

Ruthie's face lit up. "Has he learned anything about my father's death?"

She shook her head. "No. We thought the two men from this morning may have killed him, but Ryan said all they can be arrested for is arson. They were the ones who set your diner on fire."

"If only it was that easy to catch the person responsible for my father's death." Ruthie set her burger down and stared at the table.

"I agree. But murderers are often cagier than arsonists." She felt the need to vindicate Ryan's efforts.

"I'm sure Ryan is doing everything he can to find out

who did it," Miranda added.

"Oh, I'm not upset with Ryan. I'm upset with my mother, Nattie, even Chea. It seems all of them knew more than they ever told me. You would have thought once I was an adult they wouldn't have kept all the secrets."

Maxwell tossed his napkin in his empty basket. "We better get back. I only have this week to help you, and I'll have to get back to work at the mortuary."

"You go on ahead. I'll pay," Shandra waved the others off as she walked up to the bar. There were only a few locals eating and drinking at this time of day.

"That fire over at Ruthie's make a big mess?" Maxine asked, as she rang up the charges for the lunch.

"Not as bad as it could have been, but I don't think she'll be able to open for business until after the first of the year." That had been the talk she'd heard while Ruthie visited with contractors who came to give her bids.

"That's too bad. And this on top of her no-account father showing up at her wedding and getting himself killed."

Shandra handed her bank card to Maxine and asked. "Why do you call him a no-account?"

"He was a married man when he ran off, but I saw him making out up above the resort with a younger woman not a week before he left." Maxine nodded so hard her pile of hair jiggled as if it would work loose of the pins holding it in place.

"Up above the resort? Do you mean on the ski slopes?"

Maxine smiled. "When the resort first went in, in the summer the young people would hike up the cleared slopes, have a picnic and then pair off and go for walks in the trees, if you know what I mean." She winked.

"I see. And you were up there with a young man when you saw Donald Kerby and a young woman?"

"Yeah. I knew who he was because he worked for Mr. Narvel. So did my dad. He was a plumber and did a lot of work on the resort and in the old Victorian house. Mr. Kerby was a carpenter."

"Did you tell anyone that you saw him and another woman?" Shandra had told Ryan this was too small of a community for an affair to go unnoticed.

"I think I told my dad. I don't know if Russ told anyone."

"Russ who?" Shandra was making mental notes to tell Ryan about this.

"Russ Pawner, the principal at Warner High School." Maxine handed back the bank card. "I haven't told Ruthie what I saw."

"No one has told her anything. Let's keep it that way for a while yet." Shandra hooked her leather fringed bag over her shoulder and left Maxie's. She strode down the street, her phone in her hand. Best to let Ryan now what she'd found out so far.

Chapter Seventeen

Ryan waited until all the children had left the school grounds either by walking, in a car, or by bus before he entered the school. Grades kindergarten through eighth grade went to school here. The high school aged kids were bused to Warner.

The building, while not the grade school he'd attended, reminded him of Warner Elementary. The artwork on the bulletin boards outside the rooms, the desks in clusters, the smell of chalk. Even in this day of so much technology, they still had chalk boards.

He read the names of the teachers above the doors and found Chea Timms in her room. Her head was bent over a pile of papers. Her right hand making marks with a red pen. He studied her room, decorated in large paper leaves, acorns, and brown, yellow, and orange streamers.

Somewhere down the hall a door slammed shut.

Chea glanced toward the doorway and started. "Oh! I didn't know you were there. I was correcting spelling tests." Her cheeks darkened a bit as she slid the pile of papers to the front of her desk. "Did you want something?"

"I have a few more questions about Saturday." Ryan stepped into the room and continued on over to the school desk in front of Chea.

"I believe I told you everything about Saturday." She drew the papers back toward her as if they would shield her from his questions.

"I'm afraid you left a lot out."

She continued to stare at the papers.

"I've found two witnesses who saw you drive to the wedding with Donald Kerby in your car. You neglected to tell us that was how he arrived at the wedding."

Her gaze shot to him. "Who said that?"

"I'm the one asking the questions. If you brought Donald to the wedding, how did he know about it and how did you make arrangements to pick him up?" When she didn't offer any answers, he added. "And why did you pretend to be surprised he was there when you, in fact, brought him?"

She continued to stare at him. Her brow wrinkled and her lips worked as if she were trying to come up with something other than the truth.

"Withholding this information makes you look guilty. Did you two have a lover's spat behind the barn and you knocked him upside the head with a post?"

"No. I loved him." Her face paled and her eyes widened. "He contacted me a week before the wedding. He'd been keeping track of Ruthie through an online subscription of the Huckleberry Herald. He saw she was getting married and wanted to know about Maxwell. Then the day before the wedding he shows up, here, at the school, asking if I'll take him to the wedding. That he wanted to see Ruthie and explain things to her."

"Weren't you worried he'd say something about the letters and you'd have to explain not giving them to her?" He studied her reactions.

Chea nodded. "I knew I'd lose him forever if he found out I'd not given the letters to Ruthie. But he was so thankful for me picking him up and getting him out to go see her, that I thought for sure he'd forgive me."

"Why did he want to sneak in to see his own daughter? He hasn't committed any crimes."

"He said, he didn't want to take away from his little girl's day by showing up and having everyone talking about him. He'd see her and tell her he was back to be in her life." Chea's face softened, hope glowed in her eyes. "He said he'd get a divorce from Zelda and we could finally be together."

Ryan hated to squash her fantasy. "What about your husband?"

Her face became pinched and fear flashed across her features before turning emotionless. An expression he'd seen so handily used by Shandra's relatives.

"He would not have wanted me knowing my heart longed for another."

"Did your husband know you were talking with Donald and taking him to the wedding?" Ryan had a feeling the man had been kept in the dark as much as Ruthie.

"No, of course, I didn't tell him. He would have never understood my helping a man who had left his family." She peered at him as if he'd just said something stupid.

"Yet, you did."

She gave him a puzzled expression.

"You helped a man who left his family."

"He had his reasons. He didn't want them to be harmed." She thumped her red pen on the stack of papers. "He left to protect them."

"Did he tell you this when he left or when he returned?"

"On our way to the wedding. He told me how he had witnessed Mr. Narvel shoot the man his brother went to prison for shooting. That Mr. Narvel told him to leave and never come back and never speak a word of what he saw and his family would be safe and he wouldn't have to kill Donald."

"That's a powerful admission. One against a man who is dead now." Ryan switched the conversation. "How did you manage to go to the wedding alone? Well, not alone, but without your husband or your mother?"

Her eyes narrowed. "You want me to tell you I lied to them? I didn't have to. Clarence told me he had to go over the test scores with his principal and mother wanted to go in separate cars, believing I would want to stay longer at the reception than she would."

"Does your husband meet with the principal often on Saturdays?" He still didn't understand the man putting work before family.

"Like he said, they have very little time during the week to go over a long study such as Clarence has been recording." She waved her hand. "He likes numbers because they are orderly."

"And the name of the principal he was meeting?"

"Russell Pawner."

~*~

Shandra arrived at the diner in time to see Maxwell grab a man by the front of his shirt. She hurried into the smell of a doused campfire. "Maxwell, what are you doing?"

"He says he's Ruthie's uncle. She doesn't need any more pain." Maxwell continued to hold the older African American man up so his toes barely touched the ground.

"You must be my niece's fiancé. Zelda said you were a big boy." The man didn't try to get out of Maxwell's grip. He hung suspended in air, grinning.

"If this man is Ruthie's family, it's up to her to decide how she wants to deal with him. Not you." Shandra walked by and patted Maxwell on the arm. "Put him down. I'll get Ruthie." She continued into the kitchen were Ruthie and Miranda were tossing all the ruined food from the pantry into a large garbage bin in the alley.

"Ruthie, there's a man in the other room claiming to be your uncle. You might want to go save him from Maxwell."

Her friend's eyes widened, and she threw the soggy mess in her hands into the bin and hurried through the kitchen.

Shandra followed. This was a man who went to prison to protect his brother and family.

"I'm Ruthie Kerby," she said, extending her hand toward the older man.

He grasped her hand and smiled, his eyes lighting up. "My, if you aren't the spitting image of your grandma, your daddy's and my mother. She was a strong woman." His gaze scanned the gutted building. "It looks like you've got a lot of work to do here. I'd like to help, seen's how there's a possibility it happened because your daddy and me were too scared to tell the truth all those years ago."

Ruthie took a step closer to the man. "I was told I didn't have any uncles or aunts. It's going to be hard to get used to the fact I do."

"How about we go slow. I don't know how to be an uncle either, since that was taken away from me." He held his hand out to Maxwell. "How about a right introduction?"

To his credit, Maxwell held out his hand and shook. "Maxwell Treat."

"Orin Kerby. Pleased to meet you, young man. How about you show me what needs done?"

The two walked around talking.

Shandra moved over and put an arm around Ruthie's shoulders. "I think you'll find your uncle to be a good guy. From what I've learned from Ryan, he didn't kill the man he was accused of killing and he went to jail to save you and your parents."

Ruthie wiped at tears. "He looks a lot like my father."

"Come on. We need to get this mess cleaned up so construction can begin." Shandra led her friend back to the kitchen where Miranda was working away.

"What you said, about him going to jail to save us—" Ruthie walked to the pantry "—then I need to give him work here, at the diner."

"I think that's a good idea." Shandra grabbed items off the shelves, wondering if they were included in the insurance claim.

"I wonder if he needs a place to stay?"

"Who," Miranda asked, returning from the dumpster.

"My uncle. He'll be working for me, but I didn't ask him if he needed a place to stay." Ruthie handed the bucket she'd put items in to Shandra and walked toward the front of the building.

"He can stay with us if you want. We have lots of room," Miranda said, to Ruthie's back.

"That's generous of you. Don't you need to ask Alex first?" Shandra asked.

"He's been complaining about how quiet the big old house is with just the two of us." Miranda dumped items into the bucket.

Shandra grinned and said, "Do you think maybe he means he'd like to hear the patter of little feet running around?"

Her friend stood straight and peered at her. "Oh my! I hadn't thought of that. We've talked so much about his genetic disorder that I didn't think he'd want to have children until he'd found a cure."

"Maybe I should have invited people with children to the party tomorrow night..." Miranda peered off into space.

"It's too late now. I'm looking forward to Alex's surprise. Which reminds me, I'll have to leave pretty soon. I still need costumes for Ryan and me." She started dumping items into her bucket and tossing it into the dumpster. With only an hour or so more she could spend helping Ruthie, she needed to get as much done as she could.

Chapter Eighteen

Ryan had asked one of the deputies in Warner to interview high school principal Russell Pawner about meeting with Mr. Timms on Saturday to discuss math scores. As he drove up County Road 15 toward Shandra's place, his phone buzzed.

"Greer."

"Deputy Stringer. I interviewed Pawner. He said they started at ten and finished around twelve-thirty."

"Did you happen to ask if he noticed anything different about Timms?"

"He said the man was as cool and analytical as usual."

"Thanks." Ryan hung up the phone and decided he and Shandra would be going out tonight. He pushed the accelerator down on his SUV and sped up the road and her driveway.

Sheba bounded out of the open studio door, woofing at his accelerated entrance.

Shandra followed behind, her hair wet, dressed in a

sweatshirt and leggings.

He never became tired of watching her move or listening to her speak. Ryan stepped out of the vehicle and walked straight to her. "I know I cancelled our date plans, but now they are back on, in a different way."

A soft smile curved her lips and lit up her eyes. "Do these plans require me to change my clothes?"

"You are perfect just the way you are. We are going to drive to the Warner High School and see how fast we can get from there to here."

Her eyebrows raised. "Is dinner in there somewhere?"

"Yes. We'll grab something in Warner before we drive back."

Sheba started talking to them. Shandra put a hand on the large mutt's head. "And can Sheba go?"

He laughed. "Yes."

"Then it's a date. When do we leave?"

"When you're ready."

Shandra called into the studio. "I'll work on that tomorrow, Lil."

The eccentric woman mumbled something barely loud enough to be heard outside.

Shandra laughed. "All I need is my purse and I'll be ready."

That's what he liked about Shandra. She rarely put on makeup and didn't need to be fancy all the time.

"I'll warm up my truck." While the trip was more or less official, he liked using his truck when driving around with Shandra. She could sit next to him.

With a finger wave, she strode into the house.

~*~

After dinner in Warner, Shandra was full and sleepy.

She and Ryan had spent most of the leisurely drive to the county seat talking about their high school experiences. As he pulled into the Warner High School parking lot, she noted the building was new and there appeared to be a new football stadium to the right of the campus.

"Wow! Did you have all of this when you were in school here?" she asked, sitting up and noticing the smaller building to the left of the main building. The light shining on the sign denoted it as the ARTS QUAD.

"We had a two story, rock quarried building that was too cold in winter and too hot in the late spring and early fall." Ryan turned the truck off and stared at the new building. "I haven't been by here since I returned."

"No detective duties at the school?"

"None, thank goodness." He nodded toward the Art Quad. "Cathleen said they have some top-notch instructors teaching creative writing, painting, sculpting, and music in the quad."

"I might have to see if they would like me to speak to a class some time." She enjoyed seeing the excitement on the faces of youth when they discovered they had a knack for forming clay.

"Enough reminiscing. You need to pull out your phone and start timing. We have to see how long it takes to get from here to your place while pushing the speed limits." Ryan started the truck up, and she hit the start button on her timing app.

Sheba made smacking noises in the backseat as she finished the leftovers they'd brought for her from their dinner.

Sleepiness vanished as Ryan pulled out of the parking lot, not burning his tires, but darn close to it. He took side streets, avoiding the main street and stoplights of Warner. The highway to Huckleberry came into view. He didn't brake at the stop sign, only continued at his accelerated pace. Sheba yelped and stumbled to the opposite side of the cab. Soon they were doing eighty-five miles per hour down Highway 90 toward Huckleberry. The big dog had curled up in the back seat, whimpering.

At the Huckleberry city limits, Ryan slowed to forty, going twenty miles over the speed limit through town.

Shandra scanned the side streets for a city police car but found none. "Did you tell them what you were doing tonight?"

"Nope."

"Then they need to get a better night patrol out here to keep people like you from speeding through town." Which gave her a thought. "You know, Mr. Timms would have been traveling through here around noon on Saturday. There is no way he could have driven that fast through town." They were now on the County Road 15 heading east.

"True. There would have been people in the streets and more traffic than ten o'clock at night." Ryan swerved to avoid hitting a four-point buck in the road.

Sheba stood up and barked at the deer, the sound echoed through the cab of the truck.

"And there still could have been animals in the road, too." She grasped the arm rest as the back end of the truck slid on the gravel. "How fast are you going?"

"Seventy." Ryan slowed as they neared the driveway. "He wasn't seen at the wedding. He had to have come through the trees."

"From the east. Try the logging road that is beyond my

driveway." Shandra held on as he gunned the vehicle and then slowed, searching for the rarely used road.

"How would he have known about this road?" Shandra asked, as Ryan drove in just far enough to get the back end of the truck off the county road. She glanced at her phone. "Thirty minutes at the speeds you were going to get here from the High School."

"If he left the school at twelve-thirty and it only took us half an hour, he could have been here in plenty of time to see Chea turn into your driveway with Kerby in the passenger seat. The wedding didn't start until two."

"He could have driven at the normal speed and still had time to get here. I'm not sure what you were proving by going so fast," Shandra stared at Ryan. "I think you just wanted to drive fast for fun."

"No, I wanted to know if he had time to get here early enough to hide in the trees and wait for his chance to kill Kerby. And he would have had plenty of time if he drove fast. As for this road, I'm sure it shows up on a virtual map." Ryan pulled a flashlight from his glovebox and stepped out, reaching for her hand.

She stepped out and Sheba bounded out behind her.

"Sheba, stop!" Ryan ordered.

The dog stopped and cowered.

"You cowardly lion. I just don't want you running through tracks." Ryan handed the flashlight to Shandra, grasped Sheba's collar in one hand and Shandra's hand in the other.

They proceeded with her shining the light on the ground, looking for tracks of any kind.

Ryan halted. "I'm not seeing anything. Either he didn't come out here, or he had another spot he parked."

"Maybe he parked like we did. Barely off the county road." Shandra liked the idea of Mr. Timms killing the man he felt would take away his wife.

"I'll come check this area in the morning. And go back over the statements from everyone who was attending the wedding." Ryan held the driver's side door.

Sheba jumped in and over into the back. Shandra slid to her spot in the middle of the bench seat. Ryan took his place behind the steering wheel and they sedately returned to her driveway and home.

~*~

Ella came to her in a dream that night. *The chasm was gone. Left was a long flat expanse of meadow. It was peaceful. A wonderful place for a picnic. "Why are we here, Ella," Shandra asked her grandmother. The wispy woman pointed to the far end of the meadow. A person in chainmail and breastplate walked toward them brandishing a large sword. The warrior, for there was no other word to describe his dress and actions, swung the sword with great power. Another attired the same, came along swinging a spiked club. They had a mock battle, before both disappeared at the far end of the meadow. "That was fun to watch, but I don't understand." Shandra looked up to find Ella had disappeared as well.*

Shandra woke, unclear what the dream meant and feeling too foolish to say anything to Ryan. What good would it do to say two people put on a demonstration of how knights of old would fight.

"What are you doing today?" Ryan asked as they ate breakfast.

"Making our costumes for tonight. Will you have time to come home and change or should I meet you in town with your costume?" Shandra had yet to tell him what he would be.

"I'll have to let you know when it is closer to the time. My first stop is the road to the east. In daylight, I can look around better and maybe get some photos." He finished his toast and coffee and stood. "What am I going to be tonight?"

She smiled. "You'll love it."

He rolled his eyes. "If you aren't telling me what it is, I doubt I'm going to love it." He leaned down and kissed her. "What are you going to be?"

"An Indian Princess."

His eyes brightened. "That, I'm anxious to see. Bye." He disappeared out the back door and she hurried out to the studio.

She had been working on his costume last night when he'd arrived home. Lil had set up her sewing machine in the studio. They were putting together the attire for a leprechaun. She figured if she was dressing from her heritage, he should dress the part of his.

Chapter Nineteen

Ryan didn't find any tracks other than his own on the road east of Shandra's driveway. It also didn't make sense for the man to have used a fence post to kill Kerby if he'd driven to the ranch with the intention of killing him.

Wanting a better idea of the man, he headed to Nattie Small's place to ask what she thought of her son-in-law, and then he'd head to the high school and talk to his colleagues.

At Nattie's, he found the older woman hanging laundry up on an outside clothes line. She wore gloves.

"You know it could take a couple days for that to dry now that the weather has turned colder," he said, standing beside the basket of sheets and blankets.

"I'd rather let it hang for two days and have the freshness of the outdoors than spend the money to run the dryer." She hung the last pillow case and eyed him. "What are you doin' here? Do you think I killed Donald Kerby?"

"Did you hate him enough to kill him?"

She dipped her chin once and picked up the empty basket. "There was a time if I'd seen him, I wouldn't have flinched at giv'n him a lick or two upside the head. His leaving put poor Ruthie into a sadness I thought would never go away."

He hurried ahead of her, opening the door to the porch.

Nattie placed the clothes basket on the dryer and entered the kitchen. "But she growed up and became a successful business woman and found a good man for a husband." She poured coffee into two cups and set them on the kitchen table still wearing her gloves.

Ryan sat down, picked up the cup, and sipped. As he'd thought from the smell, the coffee was as strong as the batch Chief Sandberg cooked in his office.

"I'm here to discover more about your son-in-law, Clarence Timms." He noted her eyes spark before her lashes lowered.

"Clarence. You think a man who only cares about numbers would have the courage to kill another?" She swallowed a loud gulp of the strong brew.

"He cares about your daughter. He married her."

Nattie waved a hand. "He cares that they are an even number because they are married. That man told her they couldn't have children because the first one would ruin the symmetry of their family."

"Yet, she stayed with him. Why?" Ryan added this bit of information to his notepad. Why would a woman who seemed to love children, marry a man who didn't want any?

The older woman shrugged. "I guess it was better than living at home with her mother."

"You're saying she doesn't love her husband and he

doesn't love her?"

"I'm saying, I believe they have their reasons for marrying one another. I'm pretty sure it wasn't because they couldn't live without each other." She took another sip of the bitter brew.

"You don't think Clarence would kill someone he thought was a threat to his marriage?"

"I didn't say that. Remember, he likes even numbers."

"But you didn't think him capable of having the courage earlier." He was beginning to think the old woman was playing with him.

"He is very protective of what he believes is his. But how would he know that Donald would be at the wedding? No one knew."

Here he had her. "Your daughter knew. She talked with him beforehand and drove him to Shandra's."

The woman's mouth opened, then shut with a snap of dentures.

"I take it from your reaction, you didn't know about their reunion."

She shook her head but didn't say anything.

"I'm guessing, Clarence somehow found out about Donald being back and Chea meeting with him. His meeting at the high school was over in plenty of time for him to get to Shandra's and wait for a time when he could get Donald alone."

Nattie stood. "You can conjecture all you want. Somewhere else. I have work to do."

Ryan understood she was throwing him out. But why? She didn't seem all that fond of her son-in-law. Was she hiding something about her daughter and Donald?

He stood, plopped his hat on his head, and left through

the back door.

Maybe he should see if anyone at the Huckleberry Elementary School had seen Donald there with Chea. The woman hadn't been straight with him any time he'd talked to her.

~*~

After finishing Ryan's costume, Shandra called Ruthie to see how she was doing.

"Hey Shandra," Ruthie's voice sounded brighter than it had in days.

"Hi. I thought I'd call and see how things were going." She knew it would be a long process to get the diner back up and running.

"Good. Uncle Orin is a worker! And he's already showed me some drawings of renovations we can do on the diner."

"Good! I'm so glad he is in your life. Will he come to the party with you tonight?" Shandra had learned Orin was living with Maxwell and Ruthie until he could make money to pay for a place of his own. She'd thought about offering him the apartment over her studio but Lil used it for her showers.

"Yes. He and Maxwell are out looking for a costume for him. I can't believe how well the two are getting along." She sighed. "He's been telling me all kinds of stories about him and my father. All those years I went not knowing anything and now…I'm just so glad he came to me."

Shandra smiled. She wouldn't tell Ruthie that Ryan had suggested it. "I'm glad everything is going so well. I can come help with clean up tomorrow if you need me."

"I think we're good. I'm paying Orin and a couple of

men who Maxwell's father suggested. They're on retirement but need a little more spending money. People who know it's a short-term thing. Orin thinks we can find enough help and he can lead them to rebuild. It would be a whole lot Cheaper than a contractor and I won't be on a waiting list."

"That is really good news." Shandra didn't want to douse her friend's enthusiasm but she had to voice her thoughts. "I take it your uncle isn't concerned about anyone wanting to harm him or you like your father was?"

"He said everyone that was involved in that besides him is dead."

A shiver raced up Shandra's spine. 'Everyone but him is dead' echoed in her mind. She didn't like the idea coming to her. Could Orin have killed his brother to make sure the truth, whatever it was, didn't come out?

"I'll see you tonight," she said, pushing the off button and opening her laptop.

The first item she googled was ancient armor. Her thought was if she could identify the armor the people in her dream were wearing, she might be able to figure out who they were or why Ella thought it was something she should know.

Her shoulders and back ached from hunching over the laptop peering at photos. Sheba woofed at the back door. Swinging her arms and stretching her back Shandra walked down the hall and opened the back door.

Sheba brushed by her, heading for the large bowl filled with water in the laundry room shower. She made such a mess when she drank, Shandra had found it easier to clean up the mess if the water bowl sat in the shower.

"Were you chasing squirrels to get such a thirst?"

Shandra asked, ruffling the thick black fur on Sheba's head.

She was rewarded with a slobbery doggy smile.

A jazz tune drifted down the hallway. Her phone. She ran to the great room and picked it up. Ryan.

"Hello," she answered.

"Hi back. You'll have to bring the costume into town with you. I'm still over in Warner. I'll be back to Huckleberry about five-thirty."

"Okay. Do you want to put the costume on at the Police Station or at the party?" She was pretty sure she knew his answer.

"The party. The fewer people who see me the better."

"Ye of little faith. I wouldn't give you a costume that would make you look silly. Remember, I am your date."

He laughed. "That's true. I'll meet you at the party."

Before she could tell him her suspicions about Orin Kerby he'd hung up. She'd have to wait until after the party or when he was dressing to bring it up.

Chapter Twenty

Ryan pulled up to the once Narvel, now Porter, Victorian house and knew why Miranda was so excited to have a Halloween party here. She'd decorated the front yard like a cemetery with hands sticking out of the ground and witches, ghouls, and ghosts everywhere. Eyes glowed and eerie sounds played.

Shandra's Jeep was parked at the front of the other cars already here, which meant she would be one of the last to leave or have her vehicle remain here overnight and go home with him. He stepped out of his SUV and noticed the witch in the rocker on the porch moved slightly.

He wondered who Miranda had conned into waiting on the porch to scare people and hand out candy to any trick or treaters whose parents would drive them out of town to see the haunted Victorian mansion. At the top of the steps, he made as if to reach for the door and instead spun sideways.

"Boo!"

The witch jumped, shrieked, and beat him with the

broom she'd held on her lap.

"Ouch! Okay, I'm sorry." He rubbed his arm and stared at the witch who was now chuckling.

"Hazel?" He peered hard into the darkness and caught a glimpse of familiar eyes behind wire-rimmed spectacles.

"Didn't think I'd miss a chance to scare people and see who comes to this party did you?" She winked.

He laughed and knocked on the door.

"Go on in. They're making so much noise already they won't hear your knock." She swatted him in the butt with her broom.

"You're kind of fresh for a witch," he said and opened the door.

The inside was in a flurry of activity. The *Monster Mash* song played, historical figures as well as ghoulish creatures wandered from the parlor to the dining room.

The person he was looking for stepped out of the stairwell to the basement. Shandra walked toward him looking every bit her Native American heritage in a buckskin dress, beaded moccasins, and a beaded band around her head. Her hair flowed loose over her shoulders.

"There you are." She grabbed his hand. "I have your costume upstairs in the guest room."

He followed behind mesmerized by her backside swishing back and forth in the tanned hide.

At the top of the stairs, he pulled her into his arms and kissed her.

She returned the kiss, then pulled back. "What was that for?"

"For being you."

Her cheeks deepened in color. "Well, I hope you feel the same after you are dressed in your costume."

"Let's see it." He'd resigned himself to whatever she'd concocted for him.

Shandra opened the door. He spotted her clothing on the bed and next to it clothing of green and black.

He walked over as Shandra grasped his coat, pulling it down off his arms.

"A leprechaun?"

"You have the legs for tights," she said, grinning. "And if I'm dressing as my heritage, I figured you could dress as yours."

"I wasn't spawned from leprechauns. My mother's family were farmers." He glanced down at the clothes he had on. "Find me an Irish flat cap and I'll look the part."

She shook her head. "I went to a lot of work to put this together. Come on." She held up green tights.

"You do have britches to go over those?"

"Of course. I wouldn't let you show the whole world your family jewels."

He narrowed his eyes. "Where did you hear that expression?"

Her eyes sparkled. "Lil."

"She knows I'm wearing this tonight?" It wasn't bad enough so many people would see him running around in a green suit but the woman who always looked for something to hold over him, knew he was waltzing around in green tights tonight.

"Go. I can do this." He stared down at the pieces of clothing and his gut soured.

"If you're not down in fifteen minutes, I'm sending Maxwell up to help you dress." She stopped at the door. "If it's any consolation, he's in tights along with several other men. Who knew so many men had shapely legs?"

He groaned and she disappeared out the door.

~*~

Shandra smiled all the way down the staircase. She had figured Ryan would balk at his outfit, but he would put it on and be by her side. At the bottom of the stairs, she followed the merriment into the parlor.

Miranda was dressed as a damsel in distress and Alex had on a good replica of one of the Three Musketeers. They were explaining a game to the half dozen people listening. She had recognized waitresses from Rigatoni's and the nurses who worked at the clinic with Dr. Porter. She spotted Chandler, Maxwell's brother, one of the nurses at the clinic, and wandered over. He was wearing a '60s style suit and glasses.

"You look nice out of your scrubs," she said, stopping beside him.

He grinned at her. "Glad you noticed. Now if I could just get Jannis over there to notice it will be worth dressing up."

She glanced over at one of the women she knew from Rigatoni's. "Well, the way she's sending you furtive glances, I'd say it's worth it. Who are you supposed to be?"

"Dr. Martin Luther King." His voice held reverence as he said the name.

"Excellent choice."

Ryan walked into the room. The scowl on his face told her this may not be as much fun as she'd hoped. He caught sight of her and strode across the room.

Her breath caught at the sight of him in the white shirt, form fitting green jacket, black knee length pants, green tights, and black buckle shoes. He carried the top hat.

"You look wonderful!" she said, holding a hand out to

him.

He gazed into her eyes and must have seen how the sight of him affected her because he relaxed and smiled.

Ryan's gaze drifted to Chandler. "Evening. Nice suit."

"Thanks. If you'll excuse me."

Shandra watched Chandler cross the room and start up a conversation with the woman he'd been eyeing.

"Well, he didn't laugh at me." Ryan said, pulling her attention back to him.

"No one is going to laugh. It's Halloween." She pointed to Mr. Aducci wearing a string of what she hoped were fake sausages with a pizza hat on his head. "That made everyone laugh when he walked in."

Ryan chuckled. "I can see why."

"Want to join in a game?" Shandra asked.

"I'm hungry, where's the food?" Ryan clasped her hand in his.

"The dining room." She led him out of the parlor and down the hall to the dining room.

Ted and Naomi were talking to Maisie Granger, a nurse at the clinic. Naomi waved them over.

Shandra went to the group while Ryan peeled off and picked up a plate, adding food as he went along a buffet table.

"Hi Maisie," Shandra said.

"Fun party," Maisie said, watching Ryan.

"It is. Why aren't you three in the other room playing games?" Shandra waved a hand toward the other room.

"We wanted to talk and it's quieter in here," Ted said. He was dressed like a mountain man. Naomi had on a long calico dress and a bonnet hanging down her back. Maisie had on a nurse's uniform from the '50s. Cape, hat, and white dress and shoes.

"I like your costumes." Shandra felt Ryan walk up beside her.

"You two look great," Naomi said, waving a hand. "Who picked out the costumes?"

Ryan pointed to her.

"Do you want to sit down and eat?" Shandra asked.

"If you don't mind." Ryan walked over to the long dining room table and sat.

Shandra followed and was surprised when she turned and found the other three had left the room.

"They seemed to be having a tense discussion when we entered," Ryan said.

"Yeah. I wonder what Ted and Naomi would be asking Maisie about." Shandra stood back up. "Would you like something to drink?"

"Punch, as long as it isn't spiked."

She nodded and picked up two cups. The punch bowl along with other drinks sat on a table by the dumb waiter. She glanced at the square door and memories of Miranda finding the body of Dana Alvarez in the waiter prickled the hair at the back of her neck.

She ladled the punch into a cup and heard voices. They were coming from the dumb waiter and the kitchen.

"Ryan." She whispered loudly and motioned for him to come over.

He set his fork down and strode over to her.

"Listen," she whispered.

"You shouldn't be here."

She knew the male voice but couldn't place it.

"You promised everything would be all right." Chea's voice whined.

Shandra glanced at Ryan.

He reached over and slowly opened the dumb waiter door.

"I never expected Barsotti's son to be worried about Donald speaking up."

"Who is that?" Shandra asked Ryan in a whisper.

"Orin Kerby," he whispered back, his lips next to her ear. They both leaned half into the chute.

"You promised when he came back we could have a life together." Chea had become almost hysterical.

"Someone's coming." The sound of footsteps and doors closing echoed up the dumbwaiter opening.

Shandra faced Ryan. "It sounds like Chea and Orin have been in communication all this time."

Chapter Twenty-one

Ryan pulled out his phone. This was a connection he hadn't considered. He hit the dispatch number.

Cathleen answered. "I hope you aren't calling in another vandalism. All patrol cars are headed to something that's been called in."

"No. I need someone to contact the prison where Orin Kerby was being held to see who visited him and who he received mail from." He grinned. "It doesn't have to be done tonight. Happy Halloween." He hung up knowing Halloween night was the worst night to have dispatch duty. All kinds of weird things were called in.

"Do you think Orin and Chea have been corresponding?" Shandra walked toward the table carrying two cups of punch.

"We'll find out. But why?" Ryan sat down at his half-eaten plate of food.

"Maybe she hoped Donald would contact his brother and she could get information on him?" Shandra picked up her cup of punch and sipped.

"Maybe. The thing that bothers me is Chea has lied about everything I've asked her." He picked up his fork, but he'd lost his appetite thinking the woman Ruthie called a sister could be mixed up in her father's murder.

Shandra stood. "I'm going to see if Chea was invited to the party. If she wasn't, how did she know to find Orin here?"

Ryan nodded and shoved his food to the center of the table. "I'm going to chat up Orin. Something is going on between him and Chea."

They walked out of the dining room as Dr. Porter strode out into the hall, the feather in his musketeer hat bobbing.

"Oh good! You're here. I have a treat in store for everyone. I'm going to see if things are set up." He strode down the hall and out the door to the back yard.

"I wonder what kind of ghoulish thing he's set up," Shandra said, continuing into the parlor where everyone had gathered. The doors to the conservatory were open making more area for everyone to mingle.

Ryan spotted Orin talking with Maxwell. He made a line for them as Shandra headed toward Miranda standing with her parents and the Nortons.

Walking up to the two men, Ryan put a smile on his face. "I'm glad I'm not the only man in tights tonight," he said to Maxwell. The man was also dressed in green from head to toe.

"I guess there could be worse suits than the Jolly Green Giant." Maxwell scowled. When I saw the green tights, I thought I was going to be the Green Arrow or some other super hero."

"You are a giant of a man and you are happy most of the time," Ryan said.

"And you do make a cute leprechaun," Maxwell said behind a snicker.

"Yeah, well what we won't do for the women we love." Ryan would have dressed in anything Shandra asked, considering the look she'd given him when he'd walked in the room earlier.

He focused on Orin. The man was dressed as a bum. "I heard you're going to help Ruthie get the diner up and running."

The man smiled. "That I am. Her losing the diner is partially my fault."

"How so?" Ryan shifted closer to hear the man better.

Dr. Porter entered the room, clapping his hands. "My treat for all of you is ready in the backyard. Come on!"

Everyone moved toward the door to the room, talking excitedly. Ryan tried to stay to the back with Orin but the man pushed his way to the middle of the group.

Shandra was by his side. "Chea wasn't invited as a guest. She is part of the entertainment we are about to witness."

Ryan glanced at Shandra and saw she was as perplexed as he.

Everyone walked out the back door and down two steps to the backyard that was lit up with bright lights like road construction crews used when working at night. In the middle of the circle of light stood two men in chainmail, metal breast plates and helmets, holding swords.

Shandra gasped.

He glanced over. Her face had paled and her eyes were wide.

"What?" he asked, drawing her close to him to hear her answer.

"I saw this in a dream last night. These two people."

A quick scan revealed only the people he'd seen earlier were present. Orin was in the middle of the people huddled together.

"Friends and family, I would like to present for your Halloween treat from Miranda and I, two medieval knights." Dr. Porter waved his hand toward the two and they began clashing swords.

Ryan had to admit the way they moved, clashing swords and backing away from one another, then rushing and holding the swords together as if trying to wear the other out was as well choreographed as any dance. After fifteen minutes, one was knocked to the ground and the other put the point of his sword at the others throat.

The group cheered.

The one helped the other off the ground, they bowed, and removed their helmets.

A chorus of surprise went up.

Standing in the light, holding the wide blade swords were Mr. and Mrs. Timms. His mind flashed to the books he'd seen on their bookshelves. Many were on Ancient weapons.

Shandra stared at the pair. Why had grandmother shown her these two in a dream? Was it because one of them had killed Ruthie's father?

She clapped along with the rest of the people. When the others returned to the warm house, she and Ryan remained where they were. Dr. Porter was the last person from the party, besides themselves and the Timms, standing out in the cold.

Ryan led her forward. "That was excellent swordsmanship."

"I've been interested in ancient weapons my whole life," Mr. Timms said. He put an arm around his wife. "When I discovered Chea was intrigued as well, I knew she was the partner for me."

Shandra noted Chea didn't seem as excited about the whole thing. Was it because she'd used what she'd learned to kill a man she'd thought would give her a better future?

"That was a well-executed display," Shandra said. "I'm impressed with how well you can swing the sword." She held out her hand. "May I see how heavy it is?"

Chea handed her the sword the smaller woman had been swinging around and clashing with her opponent's weapon.

She gripped it hard expecting the weapon to weight a lot. Instead it was very light. "How is this large piece of metal so light?"

Mr. Timms grimaced. "I have a real sword." He handed it to her.

The weight of this weapon dropped her hand to her side, the tip of the sword resting on the ground.

"I had Chea's sword made out of aluminum. If she tried to use my sword during the battle scenes she would be winded and weak within five minutes." He nodded to his wife. "This way, we can keep the battle going and entertain."

Shandra tipped the heavy sword back to Mr. Timms and handed the light weight one back to Chea.

"But the ringing of metal on metal sounded real," Ryan said.

Mr. Timms put his sword in its sheath and took his

wife's weapon. "Here, where we strike the blades together, a stronger metal encases the blade. I aim my strikes for this to give the illusion we are clashing swords."

"This is all like a well-rehearsed play," Shandra said, watching Chea.

"Yes. We practice every week to make sure we do not forget the moves and keep us in shape." Mr. Timms smiled at his wife.

"After that great performance, how about coming in and getting something cool to drink?" Alex invited the Timms into the house. They followed him, while Shandra and Ryan took their time reentering the house.

"She had the skill to swing a post at Donald Kerby's head," Shandra said.

"But did she have enough anger to be able to pick the post up and swing it?" Ryan asked, holding the door open for her to enter.

"She isn't happy in her marriage," she stated.

"I gathered that as well. But why kill the one person who had said he'd marry her?" Ryan put a hand on her arm, keeping them in the hallway while the others were all gathered in the parlor.

"I think it was Mr. Timms. He had to have discovered Donald was back and knew about his wife's relationship with the man in the past. His own principal could have told him what he'd seen all that time ago." Shandra saw how possessive the man had been with Chea. She'd known his type and could see Chea felt as trapped as Shandra had once felt in the same type of relationship.

"We can suppose all we want. I need hard facts." Ryan led her into the parlor.

She pasted a smile on her face but her gaze sought,

Chea, Mr. Timms, and Orin Kerby. Mr. Kerby's gaze kept darting toward Chea as if he were afraid she might say something. She kept her gaze on her drink. Mr. Timms was visiting with Mr. Aducci and Maxwell.

Shandra motioned toward the bar. "Would you get me a glass of wine. I'm going to look for Ruthie."

Ryan nodded.

She moved about the room and not seeing her friend ducked into the conservatory. The lush green tropical plants seemed to have grown thicker since her last visit here. She found Ruthie in a corner on a window seat with Maisie.

"She came in with a nasty rash on her hands," Maisie said.

"Did Dr. Porter give her something for it?" Ruthie asked.

"Yes, a topical cream and antihistamine." Maisie sighed. "He told her to come back in if it didn't get better. You might want to check on her tomorrow."

Shandra walked up to the two women. "Who needs checked on?"

Ruthie glanced her direction. "Nattie. It seems she's had an allergic reaction to something."

"Ryan didn't say anything when he saw her a day or so ago." She reran their conversations in her mind. He hadn't said anything about the woman being ill.

"She's too stoic. You don't know something's wrong unless she wants you to know." Ruthie stood. "Were you looking for me?"

"Yes. How are things going over at the diner? Do you need any help?" Shandra had planned to ask Ruthie what she knew about Chea and her husband, but given she was worried about Nattie, Shandra decided to ask those questions tomorrow.

"Uncle Orin has been a huge help. With him helping me when Maxwell goes back to work next week, we should have the diner up and running by the first of the year." The sparkle in Ruthie's eyes was good see.

She just hoped the uncle didn't turn out to be another person to disappear from Ruthie's life.

Chapter Twenty-two

Shandra had opted to ride home with Ryan from the party the night before, which left her Jeep sitting in the Porter's driveway overnight. Ryan pulled up to the old Victorian house at eight to let her out.

The front yard looked like a derelict graveyard in the light of day. She wondered if Miranda would have to clean it all up by herself or if she'd hired someone to help.

"Don't go asking questions that will get you in trouble," Ryan said, kissing her before she reached for the door handle.

She smiled. "I'll try not to. I hope you get a lead on what was going on between Orin and Chea last night."

"Me too. If you're still in town at noon, call me."

Shandra slipped out of his work vehicle. "I will."

She decided to see if Miranda needed help before heading over to the diner. Before she was able to knock on the door it opened.

She and Alex both startled at the sight of one another.

"I'm headed to work," he said.

"I thought I'd see if Miranda needed help." She stepped aside to let him out.

"She probably does. While she gets excited and has a lot of energy to have a party, she's not nearly as excited about cleaning up afterwards." He strode down the steps to his car.

"Miranda!" Shandra called, peeking in the parlor and cringing at the mess.

"I'm in the dining room!"

She found her friend hunched over a cup of coffee and a scone.

"I thought I'd see if you needed help cleaning up." Shandra went to the table by the dumbwaiter and pumped hot water from the dispenser left from the night before and added some of the apple cider from a punch bowl. She sat down next to her friend.

"That was some party."

Miranda smiled. "It was fun." She patted Shandra's arm. "Thank you for coming and bringing that hot leprechaun with you."

Shandra laughed. "You're welcome. If I had known so many women would take notice of Ryan in that costume, I would have given him something else."

"The problem was, you made everything form fitting. Which, in his case, accentuates all his best qualities." Miranda fluttered her fingers up and down at Shandra. "You were also stealing men's attention in your get-up. If I wasn't your best friend and happily married, I'd be jealous."

"But you aren't because we are friends and if I had known that was happening I would have left earlier."

Shandra meant it. She didn't like catching anyone's attention except Ryan's.

Miranda sipped her coffee and smiled. "Chandler left with Jannis."

"I wondered the way they were glancing at one another. Did you see anyone else interesting visiting?" She didn't know if Chea and Orin had spoken after the performance.

"I saw Maisie talking with Ted in the corner for a long time while Naomi was visiting with Mrs. Aducci. But Ted wouldn't stray from Naomi…would he?"

Shandra shook her head. "I don't think so, and I saw all three of them in a deep conversation in the dining room when Ryan went in there to get something to eat."

"That's interesting. You know Maisie only works three days a week here and two over in Missoula with a fertility doctor."

Shandra's interest piqued. "A fertility doctor? I wonder…" Her friends had been trying for years to have children. Could it be they were resorting to a medical procedure?

Miranda perked up. "Do you think they are going to go that route to have a baby?"

"Could be." A thought came to her. "Have you ever heard why Chea and her husband haven't had children?" Ryan had told her about his conversation with Nattie and how the man liked it just the two of them. But as teachers, she would have thought they would like children.

Miranda worried her lips and finally said, "I overheard a conversation between her and Nattie at the restaurant when I first started waitressing in the evenings. Chea was crying and saying how she couldn't have children because of some procedure she'd had. Nattie wasn't sympathetic. She said something like, we took in Ruthie, no one would have thought anything of taking in another child."

Shandra sat up and stared at her friend. "Do you know if that was before or after Donald Kerby left?"

"I'm not sure. If Ruthie was living with them it had to have been after." Miranda peered at her. "What are you thinking?"

"Nothing. I'm just trying to piece together facts that will lead to who killed Ruthie's father." Shandra finished her drink. "Let's get this place cleaned up. I need to meet Ryan for lunch."

~*~

Ryan sat at the desk he'd been given in the Huckleberry Police Station because he seemed to be working more cases out of here than at his desk in the Sheriff's Office in Warner. He scrolled through the information Cathleen had found on who to contact at the prison where Orin was incarcerated to find out about his visitors and mail. His cell phone rang as he picked up the land line on the desk. A glance at the screen showed Shandra. He replaced the landline and swiped the screen.

"Hello. Is it noon?" he asked.

She laughed. "Not yet. I had an interesting conversation with Miranda this morning while helping her clean up. Chea might have had an abortion after Donald left. One that left her incapable of having children."

Ryan chewed on this for only a second. "That could make a woman angry enough to kill the man responsible the next time she saw him."

"That's what I was thinking, too."

"I'll get her medical records pulled. See you at

Maxie's at noon?"

"I'll be there."

Ryan texted the dispatcher at the Sherriff's Office to get a warrant for Chea Small's medical records. He picked the landline back up and dialed the number of the prison.

"I'd like to speak with Richard Myers, please. This is Weippe County Detective Ryan Greer calling." He waited almost five minutes before someone picked up the phone.

"Richard Myers, how can I help you, Detective Greer?"

"I would like to know who visited released inmate, Orin Kerby, and who sent him mail."

"Orin was an exemplary inmate. Why are you looking into who he had contact with outside the prison?"

"His brother was murdered on Saturday. I overheard him talking with someone who is a suspect. It sounded like they had contact while he was in prison."

Meyers sighed. "Give me your email and I'll send you the names of the people who visited him and the names of the people he corresponded with via mail and phone."

"Thank you." Ryan rattled off his county email and hung up the phone. There wasn't anything more he could do until he received the warrant for the medical records and the list of who'd contacted Orin. He left the station and walked toward Maxie's. He was a little bit early but it had sounded like Maxine had information about Chea and Donald. He'd visit with her until Shandra arrived.

As he strode down the street he caught sight of Nattie driving into the clinic parking lot. Shandra had mentioned the woman had been to the clinic once already for a rash. He wondered if it was from nerves or something else.

With his attention on the woman walking into the

clinic, he stepped off the curb and stumbled. Catching his balance, he kept from hitting the pavement. *Watch where you're going Greer*, he chided himself. He turned the corner at the post office and headed down First Street to Maxie's. It was a Wednesday and the day after Halloween.

There were still streamers dangling from the ceiling, along with a broom. Half of the room had Halloween caricatures on the walls.

"Eating alone?" Maxine asked from behind the bar.

"No, Shandra should be arriving shortly." He took a stool at the bar. "Mind if I keep you company until she shows up?"

Maxine smiled and leaned on the bar, resting her ample breasts on the Formica counter and giving him a view of her cleavage. "I never turn down conversation with a man, darlin'."

He smiled and kept his eyes on her face and not her attributes. "Shandra said you saw Donald Kerby and Chea Small having a tryst on the mountain back in the day."

"That's old news." She held up a beer mug.

He shook his head. "Iced tea, please." Ryan picked up a pretzel from a bowl on the bar. "You ever see them anywhere else?"

She poured the beverage and turned back to him slowly, placing the drink on a coaster. "I saw them more than once. They were trying to be discreet, but then, so was I." She winked.

"You were wild in your teens?" He could imagine a teenage girl with the attributes she had being a prize to any adolescent boy who garnered her attention.

"You might say, my mama taught me early that you could get whatever you wanted from a man if you knew what to do."

The bitterness in her voice didn't surprise Ryan. In his job, he ran across a lot of women who spent time on their backs, hoping to better their lot in life or score their next hit.

"Where were these discreet places you saw Kerby and Chea?"

"There used to be a motel on the north side of town that had a blind old man running it with his wife. He never knew more than one person was going into a room together. It was where the high schoolers went to fool around. We'd all pitch in for the room, one person would go and pay for it and we'd all go in."

He stared at her. "Now why didn't I know about this when I was in high school?"

She leaned forward, resting her chest against the counter. "Because you were a goody-two-shoes and wouldn't have been caught dead in that room."

Ryan nodded. He'd rebelled as a teenager but not to the extent of getting drunk or joining an orgy in a motel room.

"Did Kerby and Chea use that motel?"

"I saw them slipping into a room twice. The second time, I went out to get a smoke and heard them arguing." The bar door opened and closed. She waved at whoever came in. "It sounded like she was telling him he had to leave his wife."

"Any idea the date?" He knew it was a long time ago.

"My senior year. Nineteen-ninety-two. Spring. Can't tell you much closer than that." The door opened, allowing a rush of brisk clean air. She nodded toward it. "Your date's here."

He spun around.

Shandra smiled, closed the door, and strode toward him. "Hi Maxine."

"Hi Doll. Whenever you want to get rid of this guy let me know. I'll take him off your hands."

Shandra laughed. "He's a pretty good catch. I think I'll keep him."

Ryan winked at Maxine and led Shandra to a table. "How was your morning?"

"Busy. I'm glad I stayed and helped Miranda clean up. The whole downstairs was a mess." Shandra pulled off a stocking cap and placed it and her purse on the chair next to her. "What have you been up to, besides charming Maxine?"

"How else do you think I get information out of beautiful women?" He raised an eyebrow and she laughed.

"What did you learn?"

Maxine brought over an iced tea for Shandra and two menus.

"Thanks," Shandra said. When the woman left, she leaned forward. "Well? What did you learn?"

"That I ran in the wrong crowds in high school." His ears burned just thinking what could have happened had he been in the crowd that partied every weekend.

Shandra stared at him her brow wrinkled.

"I'll tell you later. I discovered that Kerby and Chea frequented a motel that is no longer in existence and Maxine heard them arguing spring of ninety-two."

"When he went missing."

Chapter Twenty-three

"Yes. He disappeared May of ninety-two. I'm thinking he was telling her he had to leave at that meeting." Ryan opened the menu. They didn't come here as often as Ruthie's which meant he didn't have a favorite food he could rattle off.

Shandra put a hand on his menu, pressing it to the table. "What about what I learned? The conversation that sounded like Chea had an abortion?"

"I'm waiting for the warrant to get her medical files. Pick something to eat." He went back to studying the menu.

Maxine arrived at their table. "Special today is half a turkey sandwich with potato soup."

"I'll have that," Shandra said, closing the menu.

"Why not." Ryan closed his and handed them both to the bar owner.

"Comin' up." Maxine sashayed to the kitchen.

"Have you learned anything that will help discover who killed Ruthie's father?" Shandra picked up her tea and sipped.

"I'm looking into who contacted Orin at the prison." A flash of Nattie walking into the clinic came to him. "You happen to know why Nattie went to the clinic today?"

"Last night Maisie told Ruthie that Nattie had a rash that didn't seem to be getting better."

Ryan studied Shandra. "Why wouldn't it be getting better if they are doctoring it?"

"I don't know. I'm going to the diner after lunch, maybe I can ride out with Ruthie if she hasn't checked on Nattie yet." Shandra leaned back as Maxine brought their food out and placed it on the table.

"There you go. The soup was made fresh this morning." Maxine stood beside the table as if waiting for them to taste it.

Ryan dipped his spoon into the creamy white soup and sipped. There was a kick to the seasoning. He smiled at the woman waiting patiently by the table. "This is good."

"Yes, it is," Shandra added, dipping her spoon in the bowl for another bite.

"I'm glad you like it. Spread the word that I have good lunch specials." Maxine wandered over to a table of men who had come in while they were talking.

Ryan's phone buzzed. He pulled it out of the holster on his belt and glanced at it. The warrant had come through for Chea's medical records.

"Something good?" Shandra asked, picking up her sandwich.

"The warrant came through." The first place he was headed after lunch was the clinic.

They continued eating and before they'd finished, his phone vibrated and the email from Meyers at the prison came through. Ryan opened the email and scanned the names. Early on it was Mr. Narvel and Chea who visited Orin. He'd received letters without a return address. Those had been opened and were from a person named Donald. Ryan wondered what they said and if Orin ever replied? Without a return address on the envelope had Donald put one in the letter or said where he was? It appeared he also needed to talk with Orin again.

"Is that good or bad news? I can't tell by your expression," Shandra said, putting her napkin on her plate.

"Just more puzzle pieces to put together about this case." He tossed his napkin on his plate. "Are you ready?"

"Yes." Shandra stood and he helped her put her coat on. She'd shed it halfway through the meal.

"I think I'll walk to Ruthie's with you. I have a couple of questions for Orin."

Shandra nodded. Ryan had been quiet during lunch. She knew it had nothing to do with her and everything to do with the murder he was trying to solve.

"I love this time of year," she said, breathing in the brisk air.

"What do you love about it?"

"The colors, the crisp air. Having a reason to snuggle." She put her arms around Ryan's arm and hugged.

He laughed and squeezed his arm against his body. "You know you can snuggle with me any time you want."

"But this time of year, it feels cozier."

They passed Dimensions Gallery. Naomi stood near the front window arranging a picture. She glanced out the window, smiled and waved.

Ryan nodded his head toward the gallery. "It was interesting last night. Those two and the nurse. Their conversation had been intense when we entered the dining room."

Shandra didn't like to gossip about her friends, but this was Ryan. He didn't gossip. He dug up clues. "Miranda said that Maisie works two days a week for a fertility doctor in Missoula."

"Are Ted and Naomi having trouble conceiving?"

She nodded. Ryan hadn't been friends with them as long as she had. "Naomi has wanted children from the first second she decided Ted was the one. I don't know why they haven't conceived but I think they may be taking other steps."

"Good for them. It's important to have children to take care of you when you get old."

Shandra stopped and stared at him. "Is that all you think children are good for?"

Ryan grasped her shoulders. "No. That's what my dad always said. He was glad he had so many kids so they could take care of him when he was old." He peered into her eyes. "I think children are a blessing and those who have them should cherish them."

Her heart skipped in her chest. For a moment, she thought she'd messed up again, by picking a man who hadn't shown all his true colors. But his statement proved her choice was finally a good one.

"I take it you and your father don't see eye to eye on a lot of things."

"You met him. He's as opinionated as they come and thrives on making others uncomfortable." He shook his head. "I never have figured out what my mom saw in him."

"You have all of her good qualities." Shandra leaned her head on his arm as they crossed the street.

The dumpsters of burned and soggy wood, furniture, and food had all disappeared. They stepped through the door of the diner to a gutted building. Where the ceiling had been before was now a vast open area. The whole second floor had been torn out, leaving the square stone shell and some of the appliances. There was still a bit of a campfire smell to the building but great strides had been made in getting rid of the burned material.

Maxwell, Orin, and Ruthie were hunched over a table, looking at something.

"I can't believe how large this place looks without all the walls," Shandra said.

The three spun around. Maxwell's face lit up. Ruthie had a smile, but Orin's brow was furrowed.

"I came to offer help but it looks like you are ready for carpenters and I have no skill with a hammer." Shandra stepped away from Ryan and glanced down at the drawings. "This place will look even better when you finish."

"We can make the kitchen more productive with the new set-up." Ruthie leaned over the drawing and started showing her what they had come up with so far.

"Orin, could I speak with you?" Ryan asked.

Ruthie spun around. "Why do you need to talk with him?"

"I just have a couple of questions to ask." Ryan nodded toward the door.

Orin grudgingly walked outside. Ryan followed.

"What does he want to know?" Ruthie asked Shandra.

"I don't know specifically, but I think it has to do with your father contacting him at the prison."

Ruthie's face scrunched as if she was in pain. "Father

contacted Orin at the prison? Why?"

"I think that's what Ryan is trying to figure out. You know he sent you those letters."

"That I never received." Ruthie crossed her arms. "I'm still unhappy with Chea over that. Why didn't she give me the letters? All these years, I've had such resentment toward my father for leaving without a word. If I had received the letters, I would have known he cared and was only staying away for my safety, not because he didn't like me and my mother."

Maxwell put an arm around her shoulders. "We'll probably never know. You've always said Chea kept a lot to herself."

Shandra thought about what she knew about the woman and had to agree. But she'd seemed to share everything but the letters with her mother. Why?

"And her husband doesn't seem to like her to speak about anything other than their work." The derision in Maxwell's voice drew Shandra's attention.

"You're not a fan of Mr. Timms?" she asked.

Maxwell shook his head. "That man only cares about himself and what is his."

"Ryan said he has teaching awards. How could someone that self-centered attain awards?"

Ruthie shook her head. "Those aren't his. They belong to Chea. The children and parents love her. And the school district." She looked puzzled. "Why would Ryan think those awards were Clarence's?"

"I don't know. I'll have to ask." Another thought came to her. "Does Chea like being the fall guy for Mr. Timms battle re-enactments?"

"No. She hates dressing up and being used so the little

rooster can show off his skills with a sword. But he was so arrogant, he couldn't keep anyone else to learn the moves." Ruthie snorted. "I never understood why Nattie was so excited when Clarence proposed to Chea. You can tell they aren't compatible and Chea isn't the same bubbly person I remember growing up in that household. You'll notice all those awards were before she married Clarence."

The mention of Nattie brought Shandra back to one of the reason she'd come to see Ruthie. "How is Nattie doing? Ryan said he saw her going into the clinic when he was on his way to meet me for lunch."

"She stopped by here briefly after her appointment. The man who brought her firewood must have tossed a piece or two of cedar into the cord she bought last week. She said after bringing wood in for the stove a couple days ago, she felt her hands itching. She's allergic to cedar."

Chapter Twenty-four

Ryan stood out on the sidewalk with Orin Kerby. The man wasn't being as forthcoming as he'd hoped. "Answering my question isn't going to get you in trouble with the law. Unless you killed your brother."

"I didn't and I'm gettin' frustrated that you keep insinuating that." He glanced back into the diner.

"Are you afraid your niece will start having the same thoughts?"

"Yeah. She's all I have left of Donald and I don't want to lose her."

"Then why, if you've been out of jail for ten years, didn't you contact your niece sooner? Why did you show up the same weekend as her father?" Ryan's mind jumped to a thought. "Did Donald contact you and tell you he'd be here?"

Orin stared at his feet. "Donald sent a letter to the prison, they forwarded it to a friend of mine. I gave his address when I left prison since I didn't have anywhere to go back to. I check in with him every so often to see if he knows of any work. He gave me the letter that said Donald was thinking of coming back to Huckleberry to see Ruthie. I moved in with Zelda, thinking he'd come by there. He didn't."

The man sounded sincere. "Then tell me what Donald wrote to you in the letters you received while in prison."

"He was worried about Ruthie and Chea," Orin finally said.

"What was he worried about?"

"You know. That Zelda wouldn't be able to care for Ruthie proper and that Chea wouldn't move on and get married waiting for him to come back."

"He thought she would wait for him?"

"Yeah. She was younger than him and I never saw a woman so crazy for a man. She came to the prison once a week the first three months, begging me to tell her where Donald was. I told her, I didn't know and couldn't help her."

"What happened after the three months?" Ryan asked.

"She only came back once a year on Donald's birthday, asking if I'd heard from him." Orin rubbed his hands together.

"Did she tell you she'd received the letters for Ruthie?" Ryan was still trying to figure out who had the biggest grievance with the deceased.

"Yeah. She wanted to open them and see if he mentioned where he was. I told her he hadn't said a word in my letters so I doubted he would tell his daughter." Orin blew on his hands. "Can I go in? I'm not used to this cold anymore."

"Yes." Ryan put a hand on Orin's shoulder. "If you

can think of anyone other than Narvel and Barsotti who would want your brother dead, I'd like to hear it."

Orin nodded. He headed back in and turned at the door. "You might look into Chea's husband. He visited me once. Wanted to know if Donald was out of her life for good."

"What did you tell him?"

"As far as I knew, he was."

Ryan nodded. He caught Shandra's attention through the glass door and waved.

She nodded and waved back.

He walked to the Huckleberry Police Station, printed out the warrant for Chea's medical records, and walked across the street to the clinic.

Shyanne was at the reception desk. "May I help you, Detective Greer?" Her infectious smile had to be the reason Dr. Porter made her the first person a patient saw when they walked in.

"I have a warrant for Chea Timms's medical files." He presented the warrant.

She barely looked at it and picked up the phone. "Doctor. Detective Greer is here with a warrant for a patient's records." She listened. "Yes. I know the protocol but there isn't anyone else in the waiting room." The young woman rolled her eyes. "I'll send him right back."

Replacing the phone, she motioned to the door leading to the examination rooms and Dr. Porter's office. "Dr. Porter will see you in his office."

Ryan nodded and walked through the door and down the hallway.

Dr. Porter stood beside a door. "In here, Ryan."

Since marrying Miranda, a good friend of Shandra's,

the four did more things together and Dr. Porter, Alex, had become not so stiff and formal.

"Thank you for seeing me." Ryan took a seat in front of the doctor's desk.

"Which patient do you need records on?" Alex had his hands poised over the computer keyboard.

"Chea Timms."

His white eyebrows rose. "Chea? Whatever for?" He coughed. "I guess that's your privileged information like I have to keep the health of my patients confidential."

"Yes. It is." Ryan had a thought. "Have you ever had to administer to injuries on Chea that might have been inflicted by someone?"

"You mean like spousal abuse? No. She's had a few bruises when she comes for other ailments, but she told me there were from practicing their sword fighting." He peered at Ryan. "Do you think she is being abused?"

The printer in the corner of the room whirred to life and papers started slipping out.

"I've had some conflicting information about Clarence Timms. Just thought I'd see what you had to say."

Alex nodded once and stood. He reached over to the papers that had printed and handed them to Ryan.

He glanced through them. They didn't go back as far as he needed. "Do you have any records before these? Like nineteen-ninety-two?"

He shook his head. "The clinic wasn't in existence until ten years ago and there wasn't a doctor in town before that. Everyone went to Warner for medical care."

Ryan stood. "Thank you. I guess I'll have to find out what doctor she went to before coming here."

"What are you looking for? Is it a condition that might

have come up in an exam?" Alex sat down and folded his hands together on the desk.

Not knowing much about woman things, even though he had two sisters with children, he asked, "Do you know if Chea had an abortion?"

Alex wiggled his fingers for Ryan to hand him the papers. He handed them over and the doctor flipped through the pages. He placed one, titled History, on the desk and tapped the line: Gyn: G1 P0 TAb1.

"What does that mean?" Ryan asked, staring at the letters and numbers.

"G one means she was pregnant once. The P zero means she didn't have a child. The TAb one means she had one therapeutic abortion."

Ryan scrubbed a hand over his face. "What does therapeutic abortion mean?"

"That it was done for a medical reason. There was a chance either the mother or child wouldn't live through the pregnancy." Alex had a blank expression.

"Was that the case? One of them wouldn't have lived?" Ryan wondered if that was why Chea hadn't had another child.

"It's hard to say. There have been doctors who will perform this whether or not it has therapeutical reasons and write that in the records." Alex held his hands out in front of him as if apologizing for the doctors who did such practices.

"Has she ever said anything to you about not being able to have children?" Ryan wondered if perhaps she blamed Donald and seeing him caused her to bring up anger she harbored over his getting her pregnant and leaving.

"She has never said a word to me. I think she's resigned herself to only having her students." As an afterthought, he said, "I've not prescribed any contraceptives to her."

"Thank you." Ryan got as far as the door and stopped. "How is her mother, Nattie? I saw her come in here this morning."

Alex studied him a minute. "I guess her condition has nothing to do with your investigation. She has an allergy to cedar. A different person brought her fire wood that must have had a couple pieces in it. She said she brought wood in on Sunday and her hands started itching that night. She came back in today because some blisters had grown. After scrubbing and using a magnifying glass I discovered some slivers of wood still embedded in her hands. That's why she was having such a severe reaction."

~*~

Shandra left the diner and walked back to her Jeep parked near Maxi's. She was curious about the things Ruthie and Maxwell had said about Chea's husband. She drummed her fingers on the steering wheel of her vehicle, trying to figure out how to meet up with him by chance.

The idea hit her. She'd drive over to the Warner High School and offer her services for a class on pottery. She put the Jeep in drive and headed out of Huckleberry and down Hwy 90.

At the high school, she walked into the main building. She found the office to the left of the entrance.

A woman stood up behind a small counter. "May I help you?"

"Yes. I'm Shandra Higheagle. I'm a local potter and I wondered if I might speak with the head of the art department?"

The woman picked up the phone.

"Shandra? Is that you?" Cathleen, Ryan's oldest sister, walked toward her down the hall.

"Hi Cathleen." She wasn't sure how much to let the other woman know.

"What are you doing here?" The woman was several years older than her and Ryan, but she had her mother's youthful complexion and short, slender body making her look as young or younger. Her dark hair was pulled back in a ponytail adding to her youthfulness.

"Ryan was telling me about the Art Quad here and I thought I'd volunteer to help with a sculpting class."

Cathleen gave her a hug. Shandra had to lean down slightly to reciprocate.

"Ms. Tierney is in her office in the quad," the receptionist said.

"Rachel, give me a visitor sticker for Shandra and I'll take her over." Cathleen took the sticker from the woman and slapped it on Shandra's coat. "Now you're official. Come on. Bobby loves the Art Quad. He'd do art for every class if they'd let him."

Shandra followed Ryan's sister out of the main building and across the dead grass to the newer, more statuesque building.

"Who funded the art building?" she asked, when she really wanted to ask what Cathleen knew about Mr. Timms.

"A local husband and wife who didn't have any children but loved to come to the music presentations and art shows the school put on." Cathleen stopped just short of opening the doors. "Why are you really here?"

Shandra stared at the woman. "What do you mean?"

"Ryan would have had me bring you here if he knew you were volunteering." The woman had taken on the persona of a mother waiting out a child to crack and tell everything they'd done.

She sighed. "I do want to volunteer and I did mention it to Ryan when we were here the other night—"

"What were you doing here the other night? No, don't answer. I don't want to know my brother's odd courtship rituals."

Shandra laughed. "It was business. Anyway. I was wondering what Mr. Timms was like. I thought I'd ask while offering to volunteer."

Cathleen did a body shake. "Mr. Timms is every child's nightmare teacher. He wants perfection in everything. Be it their name perfectly spaced on the top of a page to the exact spacing of numbers in their equations. My boys refuse to take a class with him. They all have to take at least one class with Mr. Timms because he teaches a required math class."

"Teachers? How do his fellow teachers feel about him?" Shandra was getting a pretty good idea of what poor Chea's life must be like.

"They all make fun of him. To his face and behind his back which doesn't help him gain respect from the students." Cathleen shook her head. "He is brilliant with numbers but he should be teaching at the college level not high school."

"Why isn't he?"

"I don't know." Cathleen opened the door. "You'll like Ms. Tierney. She's very bohemian."

Chapter Twenty-five

Ryan drove to Shandra's house unsure what his next move should be. All the facts circled back to Chea, the jilted lover. After watching her prowess with the sword at Halloween, he didn't have any qualms thinking she could have swung a limb or post and hit the victim in the head.

The barn doors stood open and Shandra's Jeep wasn't inside. Where could she be? He parked in his usual spot on the far side of Lil's beat-up '60s pickup.

As if the thought of her conjured up the woman, she walked out of the studio and met him. "Where's Shandra?"

"I thought she'd be here." He reached for his phone, hit the number one, and waited while it rang. Sheba bounded out from behind the studio, her tongue lolled out. He had to take a step backwards when she placed her feet on his shoulders.

"Hey girl, where's your master?" The phone went to voicemail. He didn't like that she wasn't picking up her phone and hadn't told him or Lil where she was.

"She not answerin'?" Lil asked.

He shook his head and scrolled through his phone for Treat's phone number. He didn't have Ruthie's and figured Maxwell would know as much as Ruthie.

"Maxwell, state your business," Treat's voice boomed.

"It's Ryan. When did Shandra leave the diner?" He wasn't too worried, but at the same time, if she had got onto the killer she could be in danger.

"She left here around three." Maxwell shouted, "Babe. Did Shandra say where she was going?"

Ryan heard some muffled words and Treat said, "Ruthie thinks she was going home. Why?"

"I'm at the house and she's not here. Lil was concerned because she hasn't heard anything from her either and when I tried to call her, the phone when to voicemail." Ryan's gut tightened with each scenario circling in his mind.

"I can go out and see if I find the Jeep anywhere," Treat offered.

"I'll try her phone again and let you know if she turns up." Ryan touched the off button and hit number one again. The phone rang twice and Shandra answered.

"Where are you?" he asked, much too forcefully.

Lil glared at him.

"Didn't know I had to check in."

The iciness in her voice told him she'd heard the same thing in in his voice that Lil had. You didn't demand anything of the two independent women.

"Forget I said that. I was worried. You weren't home, Lil hadn't heard from you, and the first time I tried calling your phone went to voicemail." He knew from the first day he'd met Shandra that to maintain a relationship with the headstrong, independent woman he would be apologizing a lot.

"I drove to Warner to volunteer at the art department."

He could tell by what she wasn't saying that the trip had been about more than volunteering. "I see. Where are you now?"

"Parked on the street in Huckleberry so I could answer the phone."

He took the hint. "I'll let you go and will have dinner ready when you get here." That would put her in a good mood. Food and her favorite wine.

"Where was she?" Lil asked, patting Sheba on the head.

"She went to Warner to volunteer in the art department at the high school." He knew there had been an ulterior motive.

Lil blew air out between her lips. "She don't stick around here long enough these days to get her work done. What makes her think volunteering is a good idea?" She stomped through the open barn doors.

Ryan headed to the house with Sheba on his heels. He'd make a dinner that would have Shandra forgiving his rash comment.

~*~

Shandra pushed the Jeep faster than usual to get home. While she'd been upset that Ryan had taken the tone he did when she answered her phone, she also knew she had done something wrong and he was going to be upset about that. She'd accepted Cathleen's invitation to Thanksgiving dinner. Ryan had come up with all kinds of excuses since their engagement to avoid a family dinner, but she felt they owed it to the family to show up for a holiday.

The barn doors were open, waiting for the Jeep. She pulled in and spotted Lil, sitting on a stool her arms crossed, waiting.

It seemed more than one person was miffed about her not checking in.

"Hi Lil. How did your day go?" Shandra asked, closing the Jeep door and walking toward the woman.

"Sunshine and horse apples." She stood, uncrossing her arms. "When you left, it sounded like you were checking on the diner and comin' home. You didn't show up by noon and no call. You didn't show up by mid-afternoon, and no call. Ryan shows up and asks where you are and all I can say is haven't heard from her."

Shandra didn't know whether to be flattered the two were worried about her or annoyed. She was a grown woman. If there had been something to call about she would have but to say she was going here then there all the time—that wasn't happening.

"I'm sorry you were worried. But I don't believe I said when I would return. You don't need to worry about me. If I'm in trouble I'll call you or Ryan." She knew enough to make sure she mentioned Lil first.

The woman nodded. "Fine. I'll wait until I see that copper thing popping out between the trees before I open the barn doors here on out." She walked away.

Shandra wasn't sure if the woman was put out or just tired and wandering away from the conversation. She walked to the barn doors, closed them, and headed to the house. It had grown dark. Shadows played peekaboo in the tree limbs bopping in the wind out of range of the outdoor lights. Her eyes and lungs stung from the icy gusts.

She pulled the kitchen door open and the aroma of

baking bread and savory soup made her stomach growl. Was that why Lil was put out? Ryan was here to make her meals when she came home late.

Sheba slid down the hallway using the rug runner to stop before colliding with her.

"Hey, girl! Did you miss me, too?"

The big slobbery tongue and cries of happiness proved she had.

Ryan walked out of the kitchen, grabbed her around the waist, and kissed her.

She pulled out of the kiss and peered into his eyes. "Wow! If I'd known I'd get such a welcome, I would have come home earlier."

"Now you know what you miss when you aren't here as we all thought you would be." He kissed her again lightly, and headed back into the kitchen.

Sheesh. It appeared everyone was scolding her for not telling them her every move today.

When they were seated at the counter, Ryan with a beer, and her with a glass of wine, and their meal, she told him about her trip to Warner High and what Ruthie and Maxwell had said about Mr. Timms.

"I've been getting the feeling that Mr. Timms knew about Donald's return." Ryan set his spoon down. "He sounds like the type who would need to know everything his wife is doing. Even if she tried to hide it from him."

Shandra nodded her head. "I agree. But I want to know, why did you think the teaching awards were for him and not Chea?"

"Because they were on the same shelf as a photo of him holding a trophy. I didn't have time to read the engraving on the awards." Ryan shrugged and tipped the beer bottle up.

"No one likes him." Shandra said.

"True. But Nattie seemed to have a tolerance for him."

Shandra stared at Ryan. "Nattie? Really? From what I've seen of her, I can't imagine her happy about her daughter being married to a control freak."

"I got the feeling when I was talking to her that while she didn't like the guy, she felt he was good for her daughter." Ryan ran the conversation with the old woman over in his head. Yes, while she didn't like the man, she definitely gave the impression he was better for her daughter than Donald Kerby.

Shandra was quiet, eating her soup and bread, sipping her wine. When she finished, she slid her bowl forward and swung her stool to face him. "I ran into Cathleen at the high school."

His senses went on alert. "My sister?"

"Yeah. She was walking down the hall when I was asking about speaking to the head of the art department." Shandra swirled the wine in her glass, her gaze on the red liquid.

"What did she have to say?" He pushed his bowl and utensils to the middle of the counter and spun. He dipped his leg, catching her knees in between his thighs.

"She said Bobby enjoyed the art classes at the school."

"Why did you leave out meeting her when you were telling me all the information you'd learned about Timms?"

Her gaze lifted. She gave him a half smile. "I didn't know how you'd feel about me running into your family and accepting dinner invitations."

His first instinct was to curse and tell her they weren't going. But he realized she wouldn't have accepted if she wasn't ready to do more mingling with his overbearing family. "You sure you want to?"

"It's Thanksgiving. That's a family holiday. You know we won't be with my mom, so I thought we might as well join your family. You said so yourself we don't hang out with them enough." She put the wine glass on the counter and leaned closer. "I've grown thicker skin and can tell your father to buzz off when I feel he's offensive."

Ryan grinned. The happiness forcing the grin came all the way from his toes. "I've wanted to be more a part of my family but didn't want you to feel awkward."

"I know you aren't going anywhere no matter what your father says. And I know you don't hold the same feelings as your father."

He wrapped her in a hug. "I am one lucky man."

She snuggled closer and he held her until his phone rang. He released her and pulled out the cell. Forensics in Coeur d'Alene.

Shandra picked up the dishes and started rinsing and loading the dishwasher.

"Greer," he answered, walking into the great room to get away from the clatter of dishes.

"Sheila Rickman. We've determined the wood I extracted from the victim was cedar. After examining the posts and limbs brought into the lab, we found traces of blood on one of the older cedar posts. The dryness of the wood explains the fine dry slivers we found on the victim. Our findings say it is the murder weapon."

Ryan's brain was already coming to a conclusion he didn't like. "Thank you. I assume you sent the findings to me in a report via email?"

"I did."

"Thanks." He hit the off button, trying to decide the best way to confront Nattie Small.

Chapter Twenty-six

"Who was that?" Shandra asked, walking into the great room with a tray holding a cup of tea, a mug of coffee, and a plate of cookies.

Ryan didn't know whether to sit or stand. He felt like he should be doing something to find more concrete evidence. "Rickman from the forensics lab. They now believe a cedar post was what was used to kill Kerby."

She stopped and stared at him. "We did have a couple cedar posts laying on the ground beside the barn back by the corral. I haven't noticed them since Saturday."

"They were taken to the lab." He sat down even though he wanted to pace the room and figure out the best way to go about questioning Nattie again. He still didn't believe the thin, older woman capable of swinging a cedar post hard enough to cause the damage he'd witnessed on the victim.

"And they discovered one of them was the weapon?" Shandra sat on the couch beside him. "What are you thinking?" She placed a hand on his thigh.

"Cedar." He stared into her eyes and saw when she connected the word with his thoughts.

"No! Not little Nattie. You think she swung that post hard enough to—to kill someone?" Her eyes widened in disbelief.

"She's allergic to cedar and while she told the doctor the itching started Sunday night, I remember her rubbing her hands together when I questioned her Saturday night." The more he thought about it. Her answers and her actions proved she told the truth and had a guilty conscience.

"Do you think when she heard about the letters from Donald to Ruthie she looked for them because she had a guilty conscience about taking Ruthie's dad from her for good?" Shandra's comment echoed his thoughts.

"It could be. But we need more proof than her hands blistering." He sipped his coffee. "She's not a threat to anyone, I'll have a deputy bring her in for questioning tomorrow morning. I don't see her going anywhere either. Her daughter and her whole life is here."

~*~

Shandra had trouble falling asleep. It bothered her that Nattie had killed Ruthie's father. Why would she take away the one thing Ruthie wanted most after spending so many years loving and helping Ruthie?

She finally dropped off into a fitful sleep. *Ella sat on the corral, pointing at horses as if counting them. Shandra walked up beside her. "Why are you counting my horses?" Grandmother shook her head. That's when Shandra realized she was counting the fence posts. "Why do you count fence posts?" Ella continued the mime of counting. Shandra glanced around and something she'd witnessed*

when she'd glanced at the body came to her.
~*~

Ryan discovered Shandra up, humming, and making waffles when he entered the kitchen. "What are you so cheerful about this morning?"

"I figured out who killed Donald Kerby. Or rather Ella showed me. I think you should go ahead and call Nattie in and ask her why she moved the post. I'm guessing she'll tell you because she thought Chea killed Donald." Shandra set a plate of waffles on the counter and handed him a mug of coffee.

"And who do you believe killed Kerby?"

"Mr. Timms. Do you have the photos you took of the crime scene?" She sat down and placed a waffle on her plate.

"In my bag." Ryan wondered what Shandra had seen in her dream that made her so positive she knew who had committed the killing. He walked into the great room, pulled the file out of his computer bag, and opened it on the counter.

He set out the photos he'd taken of the crime scene, wondering at Shandra's chewing her food as she surveyed the dead man in the photos.

"What do you see?" She pointed to the photo of Kerby propped up against the fence.

"A dead man against a post."

She shook her head. "Look at his arms, his boots, even his position."

He noted what she pointed out. "A man smashed in the head wouldn't have landed so perfectly."

"Only someone who likes things in precise ways, would have set him that way." Shandra added more syrup to her waffle and pointed at the photo with the hand holding her fork. "I would bet you a month of Sunday breakfasts that when you get Nattie to crack, she'll tell you the post was resting across Donald's lap. Mr. Timms wouldn't have been able to toss it away. He would have had to make the whole scene neat and tidy."

Ryan liked her thinking. He picked up his phone and dialed the Sheriff's Office. "Dispatch, please send cars to pick up Nattie Small, and Mr. and Mrs. Timms for questioning. Have them brought to the Huckleberry Police Station, please."

He dug into his breakfast, ready to start the questioning, knowing what his results should be.

Shandra fidgeted in the studio. She had tried for the last hour to stay focused on her next vase, but she kept thinking about Ryan questioning Nattie and the Timms. "What if I'm wrong?" She couldn't shake the feeling that they'd missed something. Unable to concentrate, she cleaned up and climbed in her Jeep. She'd go check in on Ruthie and possibly be there when Ryan called her with the news.

Ryan decided to question Nattie first. He stepped in the room with some photos he'd had Blane photo shop. The best way to trip up the old woman would be to show her a photo of the deceased with the post across his lap as Shandra had suggested.

He entered the room. Mrs. Small fit her name. If not for her gray hair and wrinkled face, one would think a twelve-year-old sat across the table from him.

"Why did the deputy drag me in now?" she asked.

He noticed she had gauze wrapped around the palms of her hands. "How are your hands? I understand you're allergic to cedar."

"Yes, everyone but that nitwit I bought wood from knows. What does that have to do with why you brought me in?" She watched him intently.

"The post used to kill Donald Kerby was a cedar post. Slivers were found in his wound." He slid the photo of the post forensics sent him across the table toward her.

"I told you and Doc Porter, I moved wood into the house and there must have been a piece or two that was cedar."

"You were rubbing your hands together Saturday night when I questioned you and your daughter."

She stared at him, her lips a tight line, her chin pointed up in defiance.

"When you couldn't stop the itching, which you were doing on the other occasions I questioned you, you went to the clinic and Dr. Porter removed small, dry slivers from your hands. The same type as were found in the victim's head."

She flinched ever so slightly.

"Small dry slivers don't come from freshly cut firewood." He stared at her a moment and asked, "Why did you remove the post?" He slid the photo shopped picture across the table. The one with the post across the victim's lap.

She stared at the photo.

"Was it because you thought Chea killed him?"

Her gaze snapped to his. "I done it. I killed the heartbreaker."

Ryan shook his head. "I don't believe you picked up a

post the size of the murder weapon and swung it hard enough to strike a fatal blow.”

“You don’t know what I’m capable of when I’m mad.” She glared at him.

“Okay, let’s say you did it. Why?”

“Because he made my daughter fall in love with him, made her pregnant, and then disappeared from her life and Ruthie’s. Then sending those letters over the years to Ruthie and ignoring Chea. He didn’t deserve to come back here and give them both false hopes.”

Her words, and the anger she emitted while speaking, made him wonder if she hadn’t hit the man. But if she had, she would have left him lying how he landed.

“I believe your anger and the fact you would have tried to hurt him…if he’d still been alive when you came across his body.” Ryan leaned forward. “I know you didn’t do this. But why did you think Chea had, who by the way, I don’t believe killed him either.”

Relief relaxed Nattie’s face, fading some of the wrinkles on her face. “Chea didn’t do it?”

He shook his head. “Why did you think she did?”

“After we were told to leave, I’d stayed and talked with Mrs. Treat, telling her I was sorry that Ruthie had run like she did. When I came out them big doors, I saw Chea coming from behind the barn. Wondering what she was doing back there, I waited until she was in her car and leaving before I sneaked down the side and I saw Donald laying there. That post across his lap. All I could think of was to hide the post. I picked it up and put it in a pile by the side of the barn. Then I got in my car and left as quick as I could.”

Ryan nodded. “That’s what I thought. Thank you for

being truthful. I'll talk to Chea to see what she has to say." He rose, walked around the table, and helped Nattie to her feet.

Out in the hallway he waved Deputy Speaks over. "Would you take Mrs. Small home?"

"Can I stay and wait for Chea? She might need me."

Ryan nodded and Speaks escorted Nattie to the waiting area.

He turned to the door where the Timmses were waiting. "Blane, bring Mrs. Timms into the interview room, please."

Ryan took his spot at the table and waited for Blane to escort Chea into the seat across from him. "Thank you, Officer Blane."

The woman's eyes were red-rimmed as if she'd been crying.

"Mrs. Timms, I have an eye witness who saw you behind the barn with Donald Kerby moments before he was found dead."

She bit her lip and cast her gaze downward.

"Why didn't he leave with you?"

Her gaze met his. "He said he didn't understand how I could say I loved him and then not give his letters to his daughter. He accused me of making Ruthie hate him. We argued. He told me to leave and he'd come see me when he could look at me and not hate me." She cried into her hands.

"Did you know your mother thought you'd killed him?"

Chea stared at him. "Mother thought…"

"You'd killed Kerby. She picked up the post laying across his lap and put it in a pile of posts hoping no one would find it, I guess. Or hoping if your prints were on it, she'd covered them up. Whatever her reason, she ended up admitting she touched the cedar post that killed Kerby."

Understanding dawned in her eyes. "Her allergic reaction is from picking up the murder weapon? Oh no! Where is she?"

"She's out in the waiting area, waiting for you."

Her eyes narrowed. "Is this a trick? You tell me my mother picked up the murder weapon but you aren't pressing charges?"

He shook his head. "She didn't do it." Ryan pulled out the photo of the body and slid it across the table. "How often do you think a man hit alongside the head with a post would land in such a well-placed manner?"

She stared at the photo for several blinks before her gaze rose to his. "Clarence killed Donald? But how? I made sure he didn't know about our meeting or that I was bringing him to the wedding."

"I'm sure your husband, being the in control, neat personality that he is, came across something that made him wonder."

"He was at a meeting. He couldn't make it to the wedding."

Ryan shook his head. "He did meet with the principal. But their meeting was over in plenty of time for him to drive to Shandra's and kill your ex-lover."

Chea's hands began to shake. "He killed the only man I've ever loved? All those years of putting up with his neatness, preciseness, and egotistical attitude and he killed my one chance to get out of that marriage?"

"Calm down and think. We've discovered there were several people who knew about you and Kerby before he disappeared. One of them being your husband's principal. Do you think he could have said something to Clarence?"

Her eyes narrowed. "I thought we were discrete back then."

"Not enough. I've talked to several people who knew about you and Kerby."

"Then I guess he could have found out from anyone. But how did he know Donald would be at the wedding?"

"Did you leave the message you received from Donald laying around?"

"That has to be it. Maybe Clarence saw it in the garbage. I know I threw it away as soon as I read it. For fear he would see it."

Ryan studied the woman. All of a sudden, she was agreeing too quickly, not sounding like a grieving woman.

Chapter Twenty-seven

Shandra walked into the diner in time to invite Ruthie, Maxwell, and Orin to lunch. They walked down the block and over one to Maxie's.

"You are becoming a regular," Maxine said as they sat at a table.

"I know, when Ruthie gets up and running, I'll have to trade off where I go for lunch when I come to town," Shandra said, taking off her coat and smiling at Ruthie.

They all settled at the table and ordered drinks.

"You seem on edge today," Ruthie said, putting a hand on Shandra's arm.

She wasn't supposed to say anything about what they suspected so she decided to ask questions instead. "Just having trouble concentrating on the next project. I need a new piece for the Winter Classic Art Show and I'm not feeling anything."

Maxine delivered their drinks and everyone ordered.

"I don't have any creativity," Orin said. "I find it

interesting when people like you, Ruthie here, who cooks masterpieces, come up with your ideas, visions."

"I'd say you have a bit of artistic talent from those drawings you made of the new diner." Shandra said.

"Those are just sketches."

"Oh, I forgot to tell you, I'm volunteering at Warner High School during the spring trimester in the sculpting department." Shandra knew it would be a stretch to drive to Warner three times a week to help out. She may have to take her break-down pottery wheel to Ryan's and live with him in Warner during the week rather than drive back and forth.

"You are going to love it and be good at it," Ruthie said.

Maxwell scowled. "Why did you go over there and volunteer?"

Leave it to Maxwell to bring that up. "Ryan mentioned the Art Quad and I thought it would be fun to work with the kids. I do that quite a bit when I attend shows near reservations. I have workshops for the kids."

He shook his head. "Nope. You went over there to check up on Mr. Timms."

She stared at him, her mouth only slightly agape. "I don't know what you mean?"

Maxwell laughed. "You can't play coy with me." He waved a finger back and forth between him and Ruthie. "We know when there has been a murder, you don't do anything just because." He crossed his arms and leaned back a big toothed smiled contrasting with his dark skin. "I'm willing to bet, Ryan mentioned where Timms worked and you learned about the Art Quad and decided to go snooping."

Her ears burned. He'd figured her out pretty well. "Ryan did show me the Art Quad before I went over."

Maxwell shot forward slapping his hands together and shouting, "Ha! I knew it."

Maxine arrived with their orders. "What's all the commotion about over here? If you were drinking the hard stuff, I'd toss you out, Maxwell Treat." She said it sternly but there was a glint in Maxine's eyes.

"Nothing. Maxwell will keep it down." Shandra gave him her best glare.

Once everyone was digging into their meals, Maxwell started in. "Why were you checking out Mr. Timms?"

"Because I've been getting differing information about him." Shandra glanced at Ruthie. "Who initiated the marriage? Mr. Timms or Chea?"

Her friend looked at her with suspicion in her dark eyes. "What do you mean initiated?"

"Did he ask her out? How long did they date? Did he propose on one knee and Chea was excited or did they just walk in one day and say they were getting married?"

"I don't understand why you need to know this, but I think they met through the Teachers Association. At some meeting when they were talking about going on strike. I'm not sure how many dates they went on. I don't remember her getting dressed up to go out at all. They were married by a Justice of the Peace a couple of years after I graduated from high school." Ruthie picked up her sandwich. "Why?"

"Do you think they married because they love one another?" Shandra asked.

"No. I think Chea didn't want to live with her mother the rest of her life and Clarence didn't like living alone." Ruthie shrugged and took a bite of her sandwich.

"But Chea seems to have put up with a lot from him. Ryan said their house doesn't look lived-in, and the way he uses her to show off his sword skills. Do you think she's happy there?"

"Chea hasn't seemed happy for years." Ruthie picked up her drink.

Shandra dipped her spoon in her soup. All that Chea had gone through because of men, she had a feeling the woman would be content to live with her mother again.

~*~

Ryan had asked Speaks to wait before taking the Small women back to Nattie's. He wanted to question Mr. Timms first. He had a suspicion the man's answers would clear up things.

He went to the room where the teacher had been waiting.

As soon as the door opened, the man stood. "Where is my wife?"

"She's in the waiting room with her mother. I have some questions for you." Ryan motioned for Timms to walk into the hall. "This way." He walked ahead of the man to the interview room.

"Have a seat." He directed Timms to the seat facing the door.

Once settled, Ryan reached over to the recording machine. "I'll be recording your answers. It's easier than trying to take notes."

The man nodded.

"Could you please state your name and occupation?"

"Clarence Oliver Timms, math teacher at Warner High School."

"Thank you. Mr. Timms did you know about your

wife's affair with Donald Kerby over twenty years ago?"

The man flustered, his face reddened, and he slowly opened his mouth. "Yes."

"How and when did you find out?"

"Why do you need to know this? It is a part of my wife's life that happened before I met her."

"The man she had the affair with was killed less than a week ago at his daughter's wedding. Just days after he'd returned to the area." Ryan stared at the man. "And had contacted your wife."

Timms face grew redder and his eyes narrowed. "How do you know he contacted my wife?"

"She told me. She said he told her he was staying, getting a divorce from his wife, and the two of them could be together."

The man slammed his palm down on the table. "No! That is a lie."

"How do you know that it's a lie?"

The man pinched his lips together.

"Okay, then tell me where you were after you left the high school last Saturday." Ryan opened the file folder and leafed through the photos.

The man took off his glasses and wiped them on a handkerchief he'd pulled from a suit pocket. "I drove to Miss Higheagle's. I thought I could catch my wife and attend the reception with her."

"No one saw you."

"There was no reception." The man stated flatly.

"But you were there to see your wife talking with her ex-lover. You saw them arguing and when she left you picked up a post, walked up behind the man, and slugged him in the head, wielding the post like one of your swords."

Timms sat back in his seat as Ryan placed the photo of Kerby's body slumped against the pole in front of him. He shoved the photo away. "I did no such thing."

"Are you sure?" Ryan slid the photo with the post laying across the man's lap toward him. "Notice anything about these photos?"

Timms flicked a glance at the photo and away. "No."

"Most victims struck violently like poor Mr. Kerby would be sprawled across the ground." He tapped the photo with a finger. "Mr. Kerby's arms are spread just so across the lower rail of the corral. His legs are together, his feet pointed straight up. And the weapon…it's place ever so neatly across his lap." Ryan studied Timms. "Looks like the work of someone who likes things neat and tidy, doesn't it?"

This time Timms stared at the photo. Ryan could tell when it dawned on the man how the precisely laid out victim pointed toward him. "I didn't kill him. I saw him and Chea arguing. But I didn't kill him. I left. I went home and waited. I expected her to come home and ask for a divorce. I knew she'd been waiting for him to come back. Her whole being changed when he contacted her two weeks ago." He glanced at his wringing hands. "We didn't have a happy marriage. She lived for the day her first love would come home. But that day, as I sat there wondering when she'd come home, I realized that while we didn't love one another we had grown comfortable in our arrangement." He looked up. "When she came home she was back to being her unhappy self. I figured the argument had been about him not wanting to marry her. I caught her crying several times, after we heard about his death. But life went on."

"You swear, you didn't kill Donald Kerby?"

"Yes."

"And you witnessed your wife having an argument with him shortly before he was killed and never thought she might have killed him?"

Timms lowered his gaze.

"You did think she might have done it. Why haven't you come forward?"

"I was happy knowing she would no longer hope for this man to take her away from me."

"But she staged the victim to look like you had killed him. In my interview with her this morning, she insinuated that you knew about her and Kerby and that you also knew they had met since his return. She made it sound as if you had made up your mind to get rid of him for good." Ryan stared the man in the eyes. "That is premeditated murder. That is a life sentence or death."

Timms gulped. "I can't believe she hates me so much that she would wish me dead."

Ryan pulled out his cell phone and dialed Speaks. "Bring Mrs. Timms into the interview room please."

Within minutes the door opened and Chea walked in hesitantly.

"Have a seat, Chea." Ryan had pulled a chair from the corner and placed it beside Mr. Timms.

She drew the chair away from her husband without even glancing at him.

"Your husband and I have been discussing what happened this past Saturday. You were correct on some points and not so much on others." Ryan laid photos of the victim out on the table in front of the two.

"Clarence did know you had heard from Kerby. But he arrived at Shandra's hoping to be with you during the reception. Instead he followed you behind the barn and saw you arguing with your old lover."

Her gaze shot to her husband. The fear pinching her features made him certain she thought he had seen her kill Donald.

"Which you said, you did argue with him." Ryan nodded toward Clarence. "He left before you did. And your mother only saw you walk out from behind the barn before she went back there and moved the weapon you had carefully placed, just like his arms, legs and feet, to make it look like a neat freak like your husband had killed him."

"He must have. Donald was alive when I left him." Chea pointed a finger at her husband.

Ryan shook his head. "No, when I asked to have you brought in this morning, I also requested a search warrant for your house. Of course, at the time I had thought Clarence killed Kerby, but I asked them to look through your clothing and the whole house for anything with blood on it. And they did find a pair of boots with blood residue in the cracks of the soles. I have a feeling it will be a match with the deceased's."

Mr. Timms turned toward his wife. "How could you frame me for a crime you committed?"

"After I hit him and realized, I'd killed him, all I could think about was getting away from both of you. Donald who held my heart all these years only to tell me he was too old to want to start over with me. He wanted to focus on his only child." Her face twisted in rage. "He had another child that I had to get rid of because he left me. Left us. I was so mad at all the ways he'd let me down, when he started to walk away, I picked up the post, gripped it like a sword, and swung for his head." She swiped at the tears pouring down her cheeks and glared at Clarence. "When he hit the ground, I thought, why not get rid of both the men who'd held me back. I propped him against the post and posed him as you would, because you can't have anything not in its place." She sniffed. "And then I walked away, hoping to rid myself of the unhappiness I've had for twenty-five years."

Chapter Twenty-eight

Shandra and Ruthie sat in Maxie's alone. The two men had gone to the diner to start figuring out how much lumber would be needed to rebuild.

"It's been good having Uncle Orin in my life," Ruthie said, sipping her hot tea.

"I'm sorry you lost your father, but I'm happy you have an uncle in your life now. I know what it's like to wonder about family you've never met." Shandra's phone jingled. It was a text from Ryan.

Chea just confessed.

She wasn't shocked that it had turned out to be Chea. Texting back, she asked, *I'm with Ruthie. Can I tell her?"*

Yes.

We're at Maxie's, she texted back and shoved her phone in her pocket.

Shandra reached over and put a hand on her friend's arm. "That was Ryan. He just got a confession."

Ruthie set the cup down and grasped her hands.

"Who?"

"Chea."

Her friend's face puckered in disbelief. "But she loved him."

"Ryan thought in the beginning this had been a crime of passion. We just weren't sure who had the rage in them to do such a thing." Shandra squeezed her friend's hands. "Do you want me to get Maxwell back here?"

Ruthie nodded as Ryan walked through the door.

Shandra texted Maxwell as Ryan gave Ruthie a hug.

"I'm glad we found the murderer, but I'm sorry it is so close to home," he said, grasping Shandra's hand and sitting down next to her.

"Maxwell is on his way," she said.

The door shoved open, Maxwell strode to the table, breathing as if he'd ran the whole way. "What's up?" he asked between gulps of air.

"Chea killed my father," Ruthie said, her voice hitched as she said father.

"Oh, baby." Maxwell pulled Ruthie to her feet and hugged her.

Shandra glanced at Ryan. He returned the concerned gaze.

Ruthie shoved out of Maxwell's arms and studied Ryan. "Are you finished with what you need to do today?"

He shook his head. "I have to write up all the reports and file the proper paperwork."

"How long will that take you?" Ruthie asked, putting her arm around Maxwell's waist.

"Probably a couple of hours, why?" Ryan's gaze flicked between Maxwell and Ruthie.

"Because I'm not waiting any longer. While you do the

paperwork, Shandra can go pack for the two of you and Maxwell and I will pack. We'll drive to Warner and get married by the Justice of the Peace with you two as our witnesses this afternoon. And we'll celebrate by spending the night in Coeur d'Alene." Ruthie gave one quick nod as if it was all settled.

Shandra grinned. "I like that idea. How about it sheepherder, can you get your work done so we can help our friends get married?"

Ryan shook his head at her and smiled at Maxwell and Ruthie. "Pick me up at three." He kissed Shandra on the cheek and hurried out of the bar.

Shandra smiled at her friends, happy she could help them finally celebrate their commitment to one another. She and Ruthie could also look around for dresses for her wedding in eight months.

About the Author

Thank you for reading *Haunting Corpse*. I had fun coming up with a story that used another of the animals at Shandra's ranch. Keep reading the series to be part of Shandra and Ryan's wedding and to see what other murders they help solve.

If you enjoyed this book, please leave a review. It is the best way to thank an author for an enjoyable read.

I love to hear from fans. You can find all my social media sites and contact information through my website.

All my work has Western or Native American elements in them along with hints of humor and engaging characters. My husband and I raise alfalfa hay in rural eastern Oregon. Riding horses and battling rattlesnakes, I not only write the western lifestyle, I live it.

Website: http://www.patyjager.net

Shandra Higheagle Mystery Books
Double Duplicity
Tarnished Remains
Deadly Aim
Murderous Secrets
Killer Descent
Reservation Revenge
Yuletide Slaying
Fatal Fall

Continued on back of page

Contemporary Action Adventure Romance
Isabella Mumphrey Adventures
Secrets of a Mayan Moon
Secrets of an Aztec Temple
Secrets of a Hopi Blue Star
Secrets of a Christmas Box

Thank you for purchasing this Windtree Press publication. For
other books of the heart, please visit our website
at www.windtreepress.com.

For questions or more information contact us
at info@windtreepress.com.

Windtree Press
www.windtreepress.com

Hillsboro, OR 97124